From the moment I turned the first page my attention was captured. Bianca Todd weaves a story that has you mesmerised as you follow the journey of two people who fall in love. The attention to detail of what life is like on a cattle property is excellent. Her sensitivity in describing the lovemaking was well written and not at all offensive. I highly recommend this novel to take on your next holiday for some entertaining reading.

~Rita-Marie Lenton
Funeral Celebrant, Author

Love in the Outback is the second book from the author in which she brings love, drama, and action to Lizzy and Benjamin (BJ) to eventually find their 'happily ever after'. Lots of emotions, with the hard trials of living on the land included, for some great reading.

~Fay Kennedy
Book Blogger

Love in the Outback was a heartwarming read that beautifully captured the charm of the Australian outback. It was refreshing to enjoy a romance set in such a unique setting, and the story kept me turning the pages. I especially loved the happy ending—it left me smiling long after I finished the book.
A great pick for fans of uplifting romance!

~Albina Porracin
Author and Publisher

I read this book in one sitting—it certainly lived up to its title, *Love in the Outback*. This is an easy read—the story flows and takes the reader along with it. I particularly like the descriptions of the outback and life in the outback. The characters are well written and you easily fall love with the BJ and Lizzy. I would recommend this book, not only for the love story and the surprise at the end, for those who would like to experience a taste of what the Australian outback, and station life is like.

~Trish Springsteen
Speaker, Mentor, Author

ALSO BY BIANCA TODD

Love After Dutchman's Road –

the first in a series of romance novels set in the
beautiful Australian countryside.

Love In the Outback – is the second book in the series.

At the time of publication Bianca Todd is working on
a number of books to complete the series.

Love In

The Outback

BIANCA TODD

*Dedicated to the men and women of the
Australian outback, particularly those
who live and work on the land.*

You are the backbone of this country.

DISCLAIMER

Love In The Outback is a work of fiction.

All the names, characters, places, businesses, incidents, and events in this book are the product of the author's imagination.

Any resemblance to actual persons, living or dead, or actual events is purely coincidental.

This book has been written using plenty of 'Aussie lingo', in the style of the language spoken in the Australian outback.

CONTENT WARNING

This book includes elements that may not be suitable for some readers:

- strong language
- violence
- trauma
- mental health issues
- sex scenes

Readers who may be sensitive to these issues should take note.

CHAPTER ONE

'Out the corner of his eye he saw an angel walk into the kitchen … she looked so beautiful, he couldn't talk, his breathing stopped. He was in awe of her. BJ had met Lizzy — his angel.'

* * *

Late January, on a Friday morning about 3 am, BJ drove out of Chilly heading for Emu Station. A new job, new life, new adventures. He pulled up and slept in rest areas on his way north-west to Emu Station. He was thankful that he had decided to bring the tent which fitted onto the back of his ute.

At Monday lunchtime BJ drove into Augustus Creek, the closest town to the station. *Boy this is different to down home,* he thought. He found a motel and got a room. Oh boy, the shower felt *so* great. BJ felt the difference in heat and humidity compared to down home. It was the middle of the day, and it was hot and sticky. He didn't know the temperature, but guessed it was in the high 30s. He changed his clothes and headed next door to the pub. He introduced himself to the barmaid, and ordered a much-deserved beer, which didn't touch the sides of his throat, so he ordered a second one. Even the beer was different to down home. He just sat quietly and looked about, observing the people around him.

Dinnertime was fast approaching so BJ headed back to the motel and ordered a meal from the restaurant there. Not a bad steak, definitely a better meal than he had been eating while driving on the road. The bed was so good to sleep in after three nights in the tent.

Augustus Creek is in the middle of the outback. At this time of year, its what's called the 'wet season' in Baines Territory. Normally it should have been raining, and the roads flooded, but this year the monsoon hadn't come.

Emu Station is in the middle of nowhere, the real 'outback'. Wickham sits to the far north, Stuart to the north-east, and Bandicoot River in the next state to the west.

The Cooee River Roadhouse lies east of Emu Station and takes its name from the river. The roadhouse and its camping grounds offer a relaxing break from a long drive. Many a traveller has stopped over for a night or two here before continuing their journey. The Cooee River also runs around the front paddocks of Emu Station and snakes its way through close by stations.

When the wet season comes — if it does — the Cooee

River floods, cutting off access to Emu Station and many other stations nearby, as well as cutting the western highway which runs from Stuart to Bandicoot River.

Like most properties in Baines Territory, Emu Station is vast and remote. The station covers about 8,000 square kilometres, and yet it's not considered large by any standards.

There are only two seasons in the north: the wet and the dry. The wet season is roughly what people living down south would call summer. It runs from November to April with daytime temperatures reaching over 37 degrees Celsius and humidity above 70 per cent. Hot and sticky as hell!

The dry season, winter to the people in the south, is from May to October, with daily temperatures around the 32-degree mark, and humidity around 56 percent. The wet season is associated with tropical cyclones, thunderstorms and monsoon rains. This year there has only been the occasional storm, no cyclones. Hopes are that another drought is not coming.

Tuesday morning early, BJ gave Jim Gordon a call, "Hi, Jim, I'm just leaving Augustus Creek so I'll see you in about an hour's time."

"Welcome to the Territory, BJ, I daresay you've found it different to down home," Jim replied.

"Yeah, I got in about lunchtime yesterday. Stayed in a motel, I thought I deserved a bed and shower after three-and-a-half days of travelling. I'm looking forward to meeting you and Sue," BJ remarked.

"No worries, be good to see you," Jim answered.

After nearly an hour's drive he drove into Emu Station. He drove up the dirt road, and over the floodway, which was the river bed of Cooee River. Following the dirt track, he drove up to the main house, to be welcomed by Jim and Sue.

"BJ, you got here," Jim remarked while shaking BJ's hand.

"Come here, you beautiful boy," Sue said in a happy voice while reaching up to give BJ a cuddle. Sue reminded BJ of Beth, and her cuddle was just like Beth's. Even though Beth was actually Bree's mum, she was a mum to many, and she cared about everyone. Beth was a caring, loving mum who showed love in her cuddles, and BJ wished he'd had the care and the love of a mother like Beth when he was growing up.

"Thanks, Jim and Sue, I am so happy to be here. A long drive, but I'm so looking forward to my new job," BJ remarked.

"I know Sue has just put on the kettle for a cuppa, let's go BJ. After your cuppa I'll show you to your cabin." Jim continued, "At the moment we have a few workers here, but today they're out checking on a few things."

"Well, work stops for no man, including Mother

Nature," BJ commented with a grin on his face, which made Sue and Jim laugh.

After the cuppa Jim showed BJ to his cabin. Jim worked all his employees hard, but he decided a few years ago to give them some comfort from the heat, especially after a long day's work. Not all employers provided air conditioning in the workers' cabins, but Jim respected his hard-working employees and knew they could do a better day's work if they had a cool room to sleep in at night.

* * *

Jim and Sue Gordon became the owners of Emu Station, when he inherited the property from his late grandfather. Jim is of average height, solid build, clean shaven, and his hair is kept short. His skin is darkened from the sun and his hands are hardened from years of working on the land. When he laughs it is contagious, and he is a straightforward talker. No beating around the bush when saying anything.

You know where you stand with Jim. He's 'old school', up at dawn, works all day, and finishes only when the sun sets. Jim works hard and he expects his workers to do the same, but he can relax when he has the time. Sue complains he needs to slow down, but he doesn't listen.

"Someone has to do it, the station won't run itself."

Sue is not tall, but solidly built, and her hair is always cut short because it's easier to care for in the heat and humidity. Fashion is just not something that Sue is into. She wears working clothes on the station, like jeans or shorts and a shirt, and she only dresses up to go to town.

She is like Jim, says things like they are, no beating around the bush, straight talking, and she doesn't tolerate fools. Many a person has unwisely underestimated Sue because of her appearance, but she will tell anyone straight if they are in the wrong. And her laugh, oh, everyone is sure it comes up all the way from her toes. She runs the main house and looks after most things about the station: hiring, bookkeeping, ordering, and much, much more.

Jim and Sue have two children; Peter, aged thirty, is a copper (police officers are called 'coppers' in Australian slang). The apple of Jim's eye is their daughter Elizabeth, who everyone calls Lizzy. At twenty-five years of age, she is slim and extremely attractive, but she is so much more than that. After completing a Bachelor of Veterinary Science degree, Lizzy realised her heart was with Emu Station, it was where she truly wanted to be. So, now she works on the station. Lizzy rides a horse just as good as any jackaroo or ringer, and sometimes better than them. Lizzy doesn't suffer fools easily and many a bloke has learnt the hard way if they have said or done the wrong thing while she is around.

Jim is not like most other station owners, he prefers the old way — employing jackaroos, station and stock managers, plus other workers. Jim hires a mustering helicopter contractor to help on the big musters.

Depending on where in the country you are and depending on the size of the farm/station, workers are called by different names. BJ calls himself a jackaroo, but in some parts he could be called a stock-hand or a ringer.

The station manager, Harry, and his family live on Emu Station full-time, and there are many seasonal workers living there during the dry. This includes the all-round labourers who do anything that is needed, like cleaning the jackaroos' cabins, mowing around the main house and, most importantly, mowing around and maintaining the airstrip.

In the outback, the airstrip is an important part of any station — particularly when the roads are flooded in the wet season — allowing workers, essential supplies, and especially The Royal Flying Doctor Service to come and go as needed. Not all outback stations have airstrips, and originally Emu Station didn't have one, so Jim had one built.

During the wet season Jim has only a skeleton staff on. He may come across as a hard man, but he does have a heart. Christmas time falls in the wet season, so he allows some of his staff to go home to their families then.

Although it is the wet season—even though this year there has been no rain yet—work still needs to be done. There are miles and miles of fences to check and machinery that needs to be repaired, so a skeleton staff is working at present.

All the cabins had their own air conditioning, and BJ was thankful for it as he could feel the heat and humidity already. As he looked around the cabin he thought, *Gee this is a bit flash.* The space had a small bathroom, a bed, a cupboard, table and chairs, and a desk for a computer. BJ thought it had all he needed, and more. He unpacked his ute and went to find Jim.

"Just wondering where I park my ute, and also I brought up my two rifles and my pistol with me. Is it okay to keep them in my cabin, or do you have somewhere you would like me to keep them?" BJ asked.

"You can park your ute under the awning behind the cabin. If your guns are in a locked box, they will be fine in the cabin. Otherwise we have a big gun cabinet in the house," Jim replied.

CHAPTER TWO

It was late afternoon when Sue knocked on the door of BJ's cabin.

"About 7 pm come up to the main house, the cook has a week off, so I'm cooking tonight," she said.

"Thanks, Sue, will do," he answered.

BJ showered and put on one of his new shirts and a pair of jeans. Rifling through his suitcase he found his deodorant. He thought, even though he'd had a shower the humidity makes you sweat, so he better smell okay. As he was about to walk out the door he stopped and combed his hair and put on the new hat he had bought in Chilly.

He knocked on the sliding glass door, and Jim waved him to come in.

"Boots on or off, Jim?" he asked.

"They are fine on, come in mate."

Sue remarked, "I hope you like roast pork, BJ."

"It's my favourite, Sue, thanks," he replied.

Out of the corner of his eye he saw an angel walk into the kitchen: average height, slim, with brown hair that flowed over her shoulders, cascading down her back and over her small breasts. She had a firm, pretty face, with brown eyes, and stunning white teeth. The white shirt she wore accentuated her small firm breasts, and her jeans hugged her narrow hips revealing how slim she was. She was so gorgeous and so sexy that the sight of her took BJ's breath away. He thought, *Holy hell, I didn't expect this in the outback!*

"BJ, hey mate you with us?" Jim remarked, looking at him and wondering if he was okay.

"Hmm … sorry, what did you say?" BJ finally answered.

Jim and Sue had a laugh to themselves, they clicked why BJ was behaving that way. "Hey, BJ, this is Lizzy, my daughter, she's a jillaroo and the veterinarian on the station." Then turning to Lizzy he said, "Lizzy, this is BJ, our new jackaroo."

"Hi," was all BJ could say. Lizzy shook his hand just like a bloke would.

BJ couldn't talk, he looked down at the floor and he could barely look at Lizzy. *Okay, BJ, get your shit together.*

"Sue, anything I can do to help you?" BJ asked.

"Here you go, BJ," Jim said, handing him a beer, "let's go outside and sit down and leave the ladies to get everything together."

Outside it was cooler now, he sat in a chair next to Jim.

"Thank you for everything tonight. I can't wait to start work," BJ said.

"I have some blokes here now, but they are over at an outpost checking on things. The rest of the blokes are expected this week or next. I know this is different for you, and you'll find I have many different characters working here. Oh, I hope you're okay with Indigenous people?" Jim asked.

"Indigenous people can ride and work better than anyone I have met," replied BJ. "Don't worry, I can learn from them."

"Oh, I noticed your reaction to meeting Lizzy. If I can give you some advice: many a bloke has tried it on with Lizzy and they have all paid a price for it," Jim said. "I know she can take care of herself so I don't say anything or get involved … unless it has gone too far. The last bloke, well let's say he left the property very quickly and it took days for Lizzy to settle down. She was hotter than a boiling kettle."

Sue called out that dinner was ready. They returned inside and BJ enjoyed the beautiful home cooked meal.

After the meal Sue asked BJ about his family, and Jim asked about the good behaviour bond BJ was under.

BJ told them he ended up on the bond because he and his mates were protecting a friend's property from attack from some low-lifes and that things got a little out of hand … especially with his friend Bree giving one of the blokes a bunch of fives and where she put her boot heel in.

"I love it, and boy, Bree must be something! You'll have to tell us more about her sometime," Lizzy said.

BJ continued on to tell them about himself: his full name is Benjamin Joshua O'Brien, but everyone has called him BJ since he was a small boy. He is the youngest of five, all boys. His mum and dad worked all the time, so his Nana Grace raised the boys and she instilled good manners and decent values in all of them. BJ was introduced to horses and farm work when he spent a holiday working for one of his cousins, and ever since then he had not looked back. BJ worked on many a farm in the Chilly district, but now work was harder to come by. He was hoping this new job would be a new adventure, a change of scenery, and a new experience, even though he would be a long way from home.

BJ also explained how he said goodbye to everyone on a Saturday night at the pub in Chilly.

* * *

Only those close to BJ were invited because they meant so much to him: Cody and Bree, Bree's parents Paul and Beth, and Cody's Dad Thomas, Rick and his girlfriend Charlie, Nick and Olivia, Phil from the produce store, Ruth from the grocery store, and Johnno and Jenny, the publicans, were already there. Unfortunately Josh couldn't be there as he was working away.

"What's going on, BJ?" asked Cody.

"You will find out in a minute, okay mate," BJ replied.

"*Quiet* you mob, shut up you lot, **QUIET!** BJ, they are all yours," Johnno's voice boomed.

BJ started, "Thanks everyone for coming tonight, I have something to tell you all. At the end of next week, I'm leaving and heading up north to Emu Station in Baines Territory for work, so this is goodbye to everyone. There is no way I could get around to you all in time, so I thought this would be the best way."

Most people had their mouths open and were in shock, and as the night wore on questions were answered.

Beth was in tears and said it was like a son leaving home, and she would miss him, and he better write to her. BJ gave her a hug and said, "Mum, thanks for everything and I will try to write. Love you, Mum." All the blokes in the group called Beth 'Mum'.

BJ didn't tell Sue, Jim, and Lizzy that Paul had said, "Well, are you going to bring home a wife from up there?"

He didn't know then that he *was* going to meet someone, and she would become his fiancée.

BJ, Rick, Nick, Josh, Bree, and Cody all went to school

in Chilly, and because they were all around the same age they knew one another well. For some strange reason after leaving school the six of them had stuck together. There to help one another, spend time together, go 4x4 driving, and so on.

Each had their own occupation: Josh, like BJ, works as a jackaroo and was currently working interstate, Nick is a builder who has built and renovated many homes around the area. Rick owns the only auto repair shop in Chilly and is BJ's best mate. And Bree and Cody, who manage Bree's family farm, announced their engagement at the end of last year.

BJ explained to Sue, Jim, and Lizzy in more detail how he ended up on the good behaviour bond.

"Last year, along with my mates, I helped Bree to stop drunken idiots from continually breaking into her farm, and other farmers' properties, and killing cows and kangaroos. We probably went a bit too far and my mates and I got put on a three-year good behaviour bond.

BJ explained all about the copper who didn't do anything about the problem and what came from it. Now with the old copper being in trouble himself, the town had two new coppers to replace him.

BJ hadn't known that he wasn't allowed to travel or work out of the area owing to the bond. When he found out he told Rick, and they notified Nick and Cody, who had also been placed under a good behaviour bond at the same time. BJ made sure they still had the phone number of Pat Conroy, the solicitor who originally represented them in court. At BJ's request, Pat successfully appealed to the court for the conditions of the bonds to be altered to allow the blokes to travel for work.

* * *

"Jim, as you know, I spoke to my solicitor Pat, and he had the conditions of the bond changed. I have an email from Pat with details of the new conditions, would you like the email for your records?"

"I've already spoken to Pat at length about that. Gee, that bloke who broke into the farms must have been on something, sounds like he had lost the plot. I'm glad you got a good solicitor. He's vouching for your good character and that's all I need. I'll deal with the police here if there's any trouble, but you don't have to worry," Jim replied.

Sue piped up that it was getting late. BJ thanked them for the meal and their hospitality. Sue said, "BJ, hospitality, gee, that is a big word out here. You get a good night's rest and I'll see you in the morning for breakfast."

BJ thanked everyone again, especially Lizzy, then he headed back to his cabin. He could not stop thinking about Lizzy. She was *so* sexy, *so* beautiful.

CHAPTER THREE

Wednesday morning and, unusually, BJ had slept in after a restless night. He was normally an early riser so he was not happy this happened on the first day of his new job. He got out of bed and went for breakfast.

"Morning, Sue, sorry I slept in. I've never slept in like this before," BJ greeted her.

"It's fine, BJ, you had a long drive up here, don't worry," Sue reassured him. "Now, coffee—how do you have it?"

After a coffee, Jim took BJ for a drive to show him around part of the property. BJ said, "Boy, I'm going to need a mud map to remember everything."

"You will be okay, mate," Jim replied with a grin.

Out of the corner of his eye BJ spotted Lizzy riding her horse. *An angel on horseback,* he thought.

"Boy, Lizzy can ride," BJ commented.

"Yes, she can. She's put a lot of blokes to shame with her riding," Jim said, smiling. "Oh, my boy, don't treat

Lizzy like a woman when she's working with you. Many a bloke has gone there and, well, let's say I have seen a few blokes eating dirt. A couple of years ago one bloke got a bit free with his hands. The other blokes just stood in shock at what happened. To this day I don't know how he drove out of here with a broken arm, a swollen jaw and a black eye. Was a sight to see though," Jim said, laughing to himself.

"My nana brought me up to respect people, especially women. You could say old-school values were instilled in me. Hearing about Lizzy reminds me of Bree: both capable women in their own right," BJ reflected.

Jim introduced BJ to the horse he would be riding there. Black with white markings on his face, this was Bingo.

"I know you can ride, BJ, but how are you at riding young stallions? Bingo was broken in last year. He was one of the wild horses we get up here," Jim said while running his hand along Bingo's neck.

"I can ride okay, eaten plenty of dirt in my time. I've been on younger and older horses. What happens up here? Will I be riding Bingo the whole time?"

"Bingo is your horse while you are employed by me. You are responsible for him, if you have any concerns yell out. As you know, Lizzy is our vet on the property. I would prepare yourself for a bit of a rough ride until Bingo gets to know you," Jim told him.

"I like to treat a horse as a friend and let them know that they can trust me. Okay for me to work with him now, or do you have other work for me to do?" BJ asked.

"You don't have any work on yet, so feel free to work with Bingo. Why don't you bring him up to the round yard near the sheds? It'll be closer than here. There's a halter for him, unless you've brought one of your own," replied Jim.

BJ told Jim that he didn't have a halter, but he had brought up his saddle and whip with him, and he asked where the saddles were kept. When they got up closer to the round yard, Jim showed BJ where all the saddles, horse rugs, and other things were kept. He told him that Lizzy had all her saddles and gear here too, and that she didn't let anyone near them.

BJ couldn't wait to get to work with Bingo.

Towards the end of the day, while riding Bingo around the round yard, BJ noticed Lizzy sitting on the top rail of the fence.

"Hi, how are you going with Bingo?" she asked.

"Hmm … pretty good. Eaten dirt a few times, but we're getting there. He's beautiful to ride and he's really responsive," BJ replied.

"Mind if I have a ride?" Lizzy asked BJ.

"Are you sure? I don't want you to get hurt," he replied out of genuine concern.

"Get off the bloody horse. You blokes think I can't do anything, Christ … men!" Lizzy replied in a determined voice. She mounted Bingo and rode him around for a bit, and then suddenly he started to buck. BJ didn't know it, but Lizzy could *really* handle herself when it came to horses. After a few bucks Bingo settled down.

Lizzy dismounted from Bingo and thrust the reins into BJ's hands. She jumped over the yard rails and started walking away without saying a word.

"Hey, I'm sorry, I've never seen a woman handle a horse like you just did. Bingo has bucked me off a few times, but you just stayed in the saddle. I'm sorry I questioned your ability," BJ called out to Lizzy.

She stopped walking and turned to face him. "No one has ever said that to me, or ever apologised for underestimating me. Hell, you *are* different from other blokes who work up here. And, yes, I accept your apology. Need any more help with Bingo, just yell out."

BJ thought to himself, *Okay suck it up mate, be kind, don't try to be anything but yourself.*

Later that afternoon Sue knocked on his cabin door.

"Since the cook and the other blokes haven't arrived yet, why don't you come over to the house about 6 pm for dinner. You're by yourself, and you need to eat," she said.

BJ was taken aback by her kindness. "Thanks Sue, but you have to let me help you. Have you cut up everything for dinner yet? If you have, at least let me do the washing up," he said.

"Oh, BJ, your Nana Grace certainly has brought you up right. Don't worry about washing up, that's what a dishwasher is for. And yes, everything has been done. I take it you eat meat and salads?"

"Thanks, Sue, yes I was taught to help around a kitchen, and I'd like to pitch in. I'll come over just before 6 pm, okay?" he replied.

BJ enjoyed sitting around the table and eating with the family, it reminded him of the many happy times he'd shared with Beth and Paul. Afterwards BJ helped clear the table. Lizzy couldn't believe he did it. She had not met a bloke like BJ, and she liked what she saw: tall, fit, black hair, firm muscles, and his face was darkened from working outside. Lizzy couldn't stop checking him out. BJ had caught Lizzy looking his way a few times and it was met with a smile and a grin.

BJ knew that the workers could use the station Wi-Fi for their computers and other devices, so on Saturday morning he sent off a few emails telling people down home what it was like there up north. But he was getting bored from not doing any real work. Even though he worked with Bingo every day, and he would clean up around the cabins and clean the saddles, he still wanted to get to some actual farm work.

BJ saw the other workers arrive over the weekend. The men differed in their ages and their behaviours: some were loud, and others were quiet and were getting on with what they had to do. He was looking forward to meeting all of them.

Monday morning early, while everyone was having breakfast at the cookhouse, Jim arrived. BJ was sitting at the front of the cookhouse, trying to be invisible, he knew he was different to the other blokes. Jim walked in and spotted him and nodded to him.

"Right, you lot, shut up and listen, and I mean listen good. Welcome back, I want to tell you all the way things are going to be this year. After the bloody shit that went on last year, things are changing. Yes, Doug, is back this year as stock manager." The blokes all let out a few words, and Jim continued, "Alright, I know you lot are not happy, but any more of his shit and he is gone. I will not put up with the shit some of you done and the bullshit that came out of your mouths either." Jim had a gutful!

He wasn't finished, "As you have probably noticed, we have a new bloke. BJ is from down south and I have already given him Bingo to ride this year."

From the back a voice bellowed, "What the hell?! I broke Bingo, he's my horse, I got him from the wild ones." It was Mickey, and he was a known troublemaker. "Come on, Jim!" he protested, while throwing BJ a dirty look.

"Okay, Mickey, this is the sort of shit I won't put up with. This is my station, I own the bloody horse, and I've fed it while you've been away. God only knows what you've been up to," Jim roared while walking towards him. "You are here to work … and work you bloody will. If not, you can leave now!"

"Why does the new bloke get my horse? Everyone knows what I did last year. Come on, Jim, Bingo is my horse," Mickey said angrily all the time walking towards Jim.

"Right, let's start the year off now. As I said, *I* own the horse, NOT you. You haven't fed it or looked after it for months," Jim said standing nearly toe-to-toe with Mickey.

"Fuck this, I am out of here!" Mickey yelled and stormed out. As he passed BJ he took a swing at him.

BJ was quick to his feet and stopped Mickey's fist. Owing to BJ's football days, Mickey landed on the floor.

"Out now!" Jim yelled at him. "You are fired. Off my station now and don't come back!"

"Your days are numbered!" Mickey threatened, pointing at BJ while he stomped out of the cookhouse.

"Anyone else with a bloody problem?" Jim yelled. "Right, breakfast is at 6 am, lunch — if we are here — is at 12 noon, dinner at 7 pm. Grog is limited. See you lot in the morning and be ready to work."

CHAPTER FOUR

That afternoon there was a knock on the door of BJ's cabin, it was Doug, the stock manager.

"Hi BJ, I'm Doug, the stock manager. I just wanted to introduce myself and have a chat with you. Can you tell me how much experience you have? Just enquiring so I know what you can do when we're mustering," Doug asked.

BJ thought, *Hmm … I don't have a good feeling about this bloke. I'm going to have to be careful of him.* He answered, "Sorry mate, but your question has thrown me. Jim knows my experience and my background. You don't have to worry about me. If you're worried talk to Jim." Doug didn't look happy, and moved towards BJ, then out of nowhere came a loud voice. "Doug, back off now, you are not in charge. You want to know anything, see Dad. This is the shit that will not be tolerated from some dropkick on a power trip," Lizzy's voice went from talking to near yelling, which brought other blokes out to see what was happening.

"Who do you think you are, woman? I'm the stock

manager and I need to know everything," Doug yelled while walking up to Lizzy. He was so close, BJ had his hands curled in fists. He thought, *Do I get in between them? No one talks to a woman like that.*

"Doug, back off … go and cool off you idiot. You don't talk to a woman like that," warned BJ.

With that, Doug started to push BJ back against his cabin when out of nowhere Lizzy hit Doug with a plank of wood on the back of the head. Doug went down.

"BJ! You okay?" Lizzy asked.

"Yes thanks, are you okay? No man speaks to a woman or treats her like that."

"BJ, thanks for getting in between, but I could have handled him. You really are different to other blokes. I can see you care about women and the way they're treated," Lizzy said.

Before BJ could answer Jim appeared around the corner of the cabins, looking like he was going to explode.

"What the hell has gone on here? Someone tell me NOW!" demanded Jim.

Lizzy spoke up and told her father what had just happened, especially about what Doug had done.

"Get me that bloody hose!" and with that Jim sprayed Doug with it to wake him up.

When Doug came to, he jumped up off the ground and yelled out, "Where is that bitch?!"

"Here I am, dogface!" and with that Lizzy's right boot landed a hard kick into Doug's crown jewels. The blokes all reacted when they saw Lizzy kick Doug: some winced, some gasped "Holy shit!" "Ouch!" Oh fuck, that would've hurt!", and some instinctively covered their crotch with their hands. Then everyone went quiet …

BJ gently reached for Lizzy's hand and pulled her towards him. "Lizzy, take a breath. Boy, you are just like Bree," he remarked with a smile. Lizzy didn't fight BJ's hand or the motion towards him.

Doug finally got his breath back and put his head up, "You bitch!" But this time BJ put his arms around Lizzy to hold her back. To BJ's surprise Lizzy put her arms around him. Well, surprised was an understatement, but he also was aware of what was happening.

Jim pushed Doug away from the cabins with the force of a dozer clearing a paddock.

Lizzy thanked BJ and asked him if she could meet him later that night. "Yep, no problem—whereabouts?" he asked.

"At the round yard, okay, about 8 pm." Lizzy said.

That night at the cookhouse while everyone was having their dinner, Jim walked in.

"Right, listen up!" Jim had everyone's attention. "NOW, with that shit that happened this afternoon … if anyone wants to know about anyone's experience, come to me. I will NOT put up with anyone threatening anyone else. Doug is off the property — never to return."

Everyone at once said, "Yes, boss." Then there was silence in the cookhouse.

After dinner, BJ showered, put on aftershave, and quietly walked to the round yard. He didn't have to wait long. He spotted Lizzy walking towards him. Even with just the evening light he could see how beautiful she was. Her trim, sexy body stirred hormones in him that had been quiet for a long time. He told himself, *Settle down, mate.*

Lizzy looked affectionately with her big brown eyes at BJ and said quietly, "Thank you for today, I have to admit to something. When Mum asked you over to the house for tea and I met you, it was hard for me. Hard because I've never met anyone like you, with manners and respect. You're very different to the blokes around here. And today when you stood up for me … well, no bloke has done that for me before. Thank you so much."

BJ explained, "The reason I didn't jump in between you and Doug is that I can see you're an independent woman and you're capable of handling yourself. But I was brought up to protect women and to treat women with respect. Some say I have old-fashioned values and morals. I'm glad you're okay though. Boy, you remind me of Bree and what she did to that bloke who came onto her farm."

They leant against the log rails of the round yard fence for a while and talked about different things, about themselves and their experiences. BJ noticed how clear the night sky was, and he commented on it.

"Up here the night sky is so bright. The stars are like a thousand lights," Lizzy said.

"The smell in the air, is that from the gumtrees? The air smells so much clearer up here. The number of different animals too … down home it's not like this. And the sounds are unbelievable," BJ commented, then added, "Hey, sorry, but it's getting on and I have work tomorrow. Can we catch up again?"

"Gee, it's nearly midnight! I would love to catch up again," Lizzy replied, smiling.

With that, they both said goodnight and went their separate ways.

The following morning while everyone was having breakfast in the cookhouse Jim turned up.

"Right, you lot, I am still pissed off after yesterday afternoon's goings-on and it's that sort of behaviour I won't put up with. I, or rather Sue, will look for another stock manager straight away So, I am 'it' until we get someone else. I will say this once, and once only, that type of behaviour will not be put up with AT ALL. Got it?!"

He went on, "For the next week we are going to get everything ready for mustering, so oil all your saddlery, and make sure the utes are serviced. You will have noticed two new trucks. Both have trailers, one is for Cookie here and all his stuff, the other is for other gear we need to take, so those trucks will need going over too. Now pull your bloody heads in and do what you are paid to do — and that's work!" Jim left the cookhouse in a foul mood, no one spoke, they just ate their breakfast.

After breakfast all the blokes got to work organising everything. Some looked after the machinery while the others completed the remaining work. A few went and made sure the roads to the campsites, or outposts for mustering, were in good condition.

Because BJ had never been mustering for the length of time they would be, he approached a young bloke called Noel, who had worked for Jim for a couple of years.

"Hey Noel, how are you going? I have a question. What do you take with you when you go mustering?" BJ asked, hoping that he didn't sound stupid.

"Good to meet you, BJ. When we go mustering take a saddle and your horse gear, water bottles, and some nibblies. I usually take a couple of changes of clothes too. Where we usually muster, there's no phone reception. Jim will give you a UHF (two-way) radio so we can keep in touch with the chopper and the other guys. I know you're new to the north, so stick with me — anything you want to know, just ask, okay?" Noel said, reassuringly. BJ thanked him and returned to work. That afternoon back in his cabin he started to get things ready.

The next morning after breakfast, even though Noel had told him what to take, BJ asked Jim the same question.

"Hi Jim, I'm wondering if you have five minutes?" asked BJ.

"Yep. I daresay you're finding it different from down home. Everything all right, BJ?" Jim asked in a concerned voice.

"Thanks Jim, yes, it's very different to down home, and I'm looking forward to getting to work. You know I've never been on a muster like up here, and I'm wondering what to take," BJ admitted.

"Hey, let's sit down, BJ, I knew you would be finding everything strange. Basically, all you need is your swag, your saddle, clothes, water bottles, a towel and nibblies, you know what I mean. Where we're going on the first muster, it's all camp-out. So, instead of sleeping on the ground we have camp beds, and cook will have a kitchen. You will be okay, BJ, I know you're nervous, I can hear it," Jim said. Then he yelled out to

Lizzy, "You got five, girl?" Lizzy walked over to them.

"You're going on this muster, aren't you?" she nodded as much to say yes. "Okay, I want you to show BJ the ropes. The other blokes know what they're doing."

"No worries, Dad," Lizzy replied.

"Thanks Jim, and thank you Lizzy. I better get back to work." With that, BJ headed for the round yard to work with Bingo.

While he was working he thought of Lizzy—how independent and strong she was, and yet how sexy she was too. He didn't know how he was going to get to know her, but he was *very* interested in Lizzy. *Okay, back to work, BJ,* he thought to himself.

CHAPTER FIVE

That night at dinner there were three new faces. BJ was introduced to Wally, Frank, and 'Old Jimmie'. Wally and Frank were in their mid-fifties and they had worked for Jim for years. Old Jimmie was in his seventies, but you would think he was in his fifties. He was as fit and as strong as a much younger man, and his naturally dark skin had hardly wrinkled from being in the sun. Sure, he had a few teeth missing, but the teeth that were there were as white as snow, and his eyes lit up when he laughed.

Old Jimmie looked over at BJ, "You worked on stations before?" he asked.

"I haven't worked up here before, but down home I've worked on plenty of farms," BJ replied.

Old Jimmie just nodded his head.

On Friday afternoon Jim spread the word to everyone, "Drinks at the cookhouse at 5pm, barbecue 6 pm."

Later at the cookhouse, BJ said hi to everybody, grabbed a stubbie, and then sat away from everyone, quietly watching them. He was trying to figure out each bloke's character when Jim, Sue, and Lizzy arrived. Sue came over to him, "Now how is everything, BJ?"

"Everything's okay, thanks Sue. It's good of you and Jim to put on this barbecue, I'm enjoying having a beer and a steak and a chance to unwind for a bit."

During the night he continued to check everyone out, including Lizzy … she was so sexy in her tight jeans. It was then he noticed the big shiny buckle on her belt, so he went over to her and asked her about it.

"I won it last year for barrel racing at a rodeo," she explained.

BJ told Lizzy about how Bree used to compete in barrel racing too, but now she no longer participated. He explained that the bloke Bree had been seeing had beaten her up because she was congratulated by *other men* for winning the barrel racing buckle. His behaviour and his treatment of Bree caused her trauma, but through counselling and the help of loving friends and family she had pulled through. The bloke was a real mongrel and didn't have any respect for women.

They were conscious of being seen to spend too much time together at the barbecue so they deliberately mixed with other groups, exchanging careful glances now and then, and sometimes winking at one another, hoping no one saw them. They didn't know that Jim and Sue saw them and suspected something was going on between BJ and Lizzy, but they decided to leave well enough alone.

The next day, Saturday, was a day off and BJ met up with Lizzy at the round yard. They saddled up their horses, this would be a test for Bingo. Lizzy led the way down to the river. They talked easily about this and that and enjoyed the ride. BJ was loving it, not only learning about the outback, but he was also getting to know Lizzy.

They came near to what they called the swimming hole. Lizzy stopped and grabbed her rifle; she had spotted a large crocodile sunning itself on the opposite river bank.

"BJ, I want you to slowly back up. See over there, a big croc (Aussie slang for crocodile)," she said nervously.

They backed up, and when Lizzy thought they were far enough away she grabbed her UHF radio.

"Dad, you on air?" she asked.

"Yes, what's the matter?" Jim asked, concerned.

"I'm down at the swimming hole, and we have a big croc here. You need to ring Old Champ and get him down here. It wasn't happy to see me," she said calmly, all the time watching the croc.

"Okay will do, you get the bloody hell out of there. I'll let everyone know the swimming hole is out because of the croc," Jim said.

Lizzy and BJ slowly left the area. They continued their ride until they got up to an old house. "No one lives here, we don't use it at all. Want to stretch your legs?" Lizzy asked.

BJ dismounted from Bingo and walked around. After tying up the horses, they found a shady spot to sit down together and have a drink. BJ knew that he had to say something, and now was the time.

"Lizzy, you're a strong, independent woman. You stand up for yourself, you know what you want. I can see you're a great horsewoman and, boy, can you ride! And … honestly … you're very attractive and very sexy, but there's one thing I *don't* know about you. I don't mean to be rude by asking, but do you have a boyfriend?"

"No, I've not had a boyfriend, I went to uni, came home to work on the station, and this is where I want to be. And besides, well, I hadn't met the right bloke. *But I think I might have met him now!*" she said.

The last bit took BJ by surprise and he choked on the drink of water he had just taken. Lizzy laughed.

BJ responded, "You said you don't want to be treated like a woman when we're mustering. I can understand that. I don't want to do anything to cross that line. I haven't had a girlfriend for a long time. I just haven't met the right person. *But, like you, I think I've met the right person now.*"

They both looked at the ground and grinned, then for a brief moment Lizzy leaned into BJ. It was a moment in time that BJ couldn't stop thinking about afterwards. When they got back to the round yard they agreed they would catch up later. BJ hoped he hadn't ruined his chance to get to know Lizzy *much* better.

Over the next couple of weeks all the gear and trucks were organised for mustering. Jim and all the jackaroos and Lizzy and Cookie left on a 'short' muster. At night BJ and Lizzy would sit next to one another with the other workers around the campfire. One night while it was just them and a couple of other workers, BJ whispered to Lizzy, "Okay if I put my arm behind you?"

She said yes, and asked if it was okay for her to do the same. BJ smiled. It wasn't much, but it felt good. He thought how much he wanted Lizzy. When she responded and put her arm around BJ it felt so good to feel someone's touch.

On another night they were sitting on the log around the campfire, and most of the blokes had turned in for the night. They were laughing about something when Lizzy put her arm behind BJ. He wasn't ready for the feel of her hand on the bare of his back. To his surprise Lizzy had pulled his shirt out of his jeans and put her hand on his warm, bare skin. He smiled at Lizzy as if to say, 'I like that'. He whispered to her, "Can I do the same?" Very quietly she said yes.

The feel of her skin, was so soft and so smooth. BJ had to remind himself not to get carried away. Slow steps. Their closeness and their laughter hadn't gone unnoticed by the other blokes. A couple of them had said a few words about it and Lizzy responded with a stare. Jim had noticed too, but all he did was watch. Often they would sit and talk when everyone had gone to bed or into their swags. They were becoming more comfortable with each other and sometimes their bodies would make contact; the feel of her body against his felt so right he didn't want it to stop. Often Lizzy would whisper something to BJ, and it made him smile.

BJ was starting to have real feelings for Lizzy, yet he was careful. When they were together he showed Lizzy he cared for her and that he wanted to really get to know her. But while mustering and when he was around the other blokes he didn't show anything. Everyone got stuck in and did the work that was required. Days turned into weeks, and this was only a short muster!

Finally, back at the main house, time to wash all the gear, do maintenance on the trucks and saddles, and be ready to head out again for the next muster.

One morning Lizzy asked to talk to Sue about something. *What's wrong,* Sue wondered.

"Mum, how did you know Dad was the right bloke for

you?" Lizzy asked seriously. Sue was taken aback by the question.

"Well … I met your dad when I was working in a café in Stuart. We both knew there was something from the start," Sue replied.

"Did you fall in love with Dad quickly?"

Sue gave a little laugh, "We both fell in love with each other quickly, and we knew we wanted to be together. Why do you ask that? What's going on, Lizzy?"

"I have never had the feelings I'm having at the moment. I think I'm falling in love with BJ, but I don't know what to do about it or what to say to him," she replied.

"Liz, Dad and I picked up something the night BJ arrived. We're not blind. Remember one thing: you have to work with him. You've seen Dad and me argue—no relationship goes without arguments. It's how you deal with them and how you resolve them that matters."

"Like Dad, he just walks away?" Lizzy said.

"Yes, and that makes me so mad and, no, that doesn't help. Don't forget that your Dad and I are here for you, okay?" Sue said.

That night when Jim and Sue were sitting out on the verandah having a beer, she told him about the talk with Lizzy. Jim grinned and broke into laughter.

"You missed what went on of a night time on the

muster. They thought I was asleep." He laughed and then continued, "They sat around the fire and talked. They would put an arm around each other and think no one would notice. Looks like I was right, I'm sure there's something going on between them. I know the other blokes have started to make jokes about them. Oh, how have you been getting on hiring a new stock manager?"

"Boy, what a job there! I have a bloke coming next week. Not married, no kids. I worry about him with Lizzy though. He had trouble at his last job, but I can't find out any information about it." Sue said.

"Well, if any shit goes on its OUT the bloody front gate quicker than a blue-arsed fly!" Jim stated, and then he said he was hitting the hay as he got up to go to bed.

CHAPTER SIX

On Sunday morning, Kevin, the new stock manager arrived.

Sue greeted him and showed him to the small house he was to stay in. He asked about the help around the house, in particular who would clean and do his laundry. Sue was taken aback by this, and in a very firm voice said, "**You!**" He wasn't happy about that.

Kevin was tall with brown hair, not skinny but not too solid either. He didn't look like he had ever done a hard day's work in his life.

At dinner that night Jim introduced him to everyone. Some of the blokes made the comment amongst themselves, "Wonder if he's ever done a day's hard work?" They were meaning he looked out of place, too well dressed. And even more, they wondered how long he would be on the station for.

They didn't have to wait long to see what happened.

Kevin was always at Jim's and Sue's house, which was known as the main house, and they noticed that he was giving Lizzy a lot of attention. And Jim was starting to become concerned about Kevin's ability to be stock manager.

On Tuesday afternoon Kevin was having a coffee with Jim at the main house. "Kevin, I'm not blind, and I'll tell you this only once. Lizzy makes her own choices, and if you cross a line with her you won't be on the station long. Got me?" Jim said, then continued, "There is no reason for you to be here all the time, so go and do your job. Oh … and on my station grog is limited, so put the lot you brought with you in the grog fridge at the cookhouse."

Kevin was surprised by the warning from Jim. He liked Lizzy and wanted to continue to see her and talk with her.

In late May it came time to head out on the next muster. This was a big muster, and Jim had hoped to be heading out on this long muster before now. When they did leave, the muster crew was made up of Jim, Cookie and one of his offsiders, most of the jackaroos, Lizzy, of course, and some others.

This muster was much larger than the previous one. It was further away from the main house and a lot of work was needed to be done during it. Jim would be selling a lot of the stock brought in from this muster.

Naturally, the camp was bigger this time and had a lot more to it. It had a shed for the 'cookhouse' and for everyone to eat in. There was also a long shed with wire camp beds for the workers to put their swags on, so they wouldn't be sleeping on the ground. Even so, because of the heat and humidity some workers preferred to sleep outdoors. But they would always check their swags for any snakes or other animals before turning in for the night! There was a small portable building with four 'drop' toilets in it: holes dug in the earth with a toilet seat on a bench over the hole. The showers had cold water only, and were made up of wooden boards on the ground, with tarps — or in most places hessian material — hung around three posts for privacy. The shower heads hung from rails which came up from the ground at the back of the shower.

Because there had been no rain the dam was low and the water in it was not suitable for drinking. So, the water for showering and for the cook to use was stored in a large tank. Jim had one of the workers fill the tank with water prior to the muster, and it was Cookie's job to keep an eye on the water level in it. There was also a generator which ran the fridge and lights.

This time Jim hired a chopper (helicopter) mustering company to help bring in the cattle from further out, and to help with pushing the cattle down the lane to the stockyards, which had been erected many years ago. The stockyards consisted of many yards of various sizes depending on whether they would be holding cattle or calves in them.

The gates—which were brought from the main house—made up a 'poddy' pen. A 'poddy' calf is a calf that is being raised by hand, usually because it has lost its mother. Some calves would lose their mothers during mustering, and if one of the workers didn't look after them the calves would die. The poddies would be taken back to the main house to be raised and then released.

BJ was amazed at the skill of the chopper pilots. Weaving to and fro close to the ground, the chopper nearly on its side, the nose barely above the dirt.

A herd of cattle was being pushed down the lane toward the yards when one young bull decided to jump the hessian wrap which had been hung to hide the workers and the open plain. Up he went and he didn't clear the fence, instead he pushed it over and headed off to the open paddock. With some skill, Old Jimmie was flying on his horse after him. BJ and another worker quickly followed Old Jimmie.

Riding full canter, sliding out of the saddle and down one side so they would miss a tree branch. Jumping over old logs. They caught up with the bull and started to turn it back towards the yards when suddenly Bingo reared up. Old Jimmie yelled out to BJ, "Watch out—snake!" With that, BJ pulled on Bingo's reins to bring him to a halt and then pulled back on the reins for Bingo to backup. When he stopped he looked, and the snake was still there in an attacking position. He was too far away to use his whip to deal with the snake, so he got his pistol out and—with dead-eye precision—the snake was dead.

Old Jimmie rode up to the now-dead snake and said, "You killed it BJ, I'll have it for dinner tonight."

In the outback, Indigenous people eat a range of animals, including snake. Old Jimmie was happy. He made sure the 'Joe Blake'—the Australian slang for snake—was indeed dead, and put it in a bag on his saddle. The other jackaroos had herded the bull back to the yards. Shortly afterwards, BJ and Old Jimmie arrived at the yards and were met by Jim.

"Well, what have you two been up to?" he enquired. Old Jimmie told Jim what had happened and then he returned to the yards with his evening meal.

During the draft many a worker had to make a sudden jump up and over the fence because of cattle with bad attitudes. Whether it was a cow or a bull, it was probably a bush cow (wild one), they were always off to the meat works. The workers in the yards had to have eyes in the backs of their heads. There was no noise as bad as the snort from a bull just behind you to make you jump the nearest rail.

There are usually no days off while on the big muster. The first couple of days were a learning experience for BJ, and he was loving it, even though it was hard work and it was dusty and hot. By night time everyone was buggered and fell into their swags and slept until early morning. Lizzy and BJ managed to get some time together to talk, and they continued to enjoy each other's company.

One day while drafting cattle in the yard, Kevin was not paying attention and didn't see there was a bull behind him. Suddenly he was thrown out of the yard by the bull! Work stopped so they could see if he was alright. Old Jimmie commented, "You too slow, that bull got you. You had wings the way you flew over the rails." This was met with laughter from everyone else, but not from Kevin.

"You lot shut the hell up and get back to work!" he barked at them; his ego was more bruised than his backside.

That night Lizzy didn't sit and talk with BJ, instead Kevin sat with her. The next day he was with her on the muster too. For the first time BJ felt something he had not felt before: jealousy. He had developed strong feelings for Lizzy and he had intended to tell her, but Kevin interrupted that plan.

One night around the campfire, BJ overheard Kevin. "Lizzy is so beautiful, I can't stop looking at her. You wait, she'll become my wife, and I'll run the station."

BJ thought, *What the fark! Mate you are so full of it. Jim would never allow you to do that.* He knew then he had to tell Lizzy how he felt.

"Hey, Lizzy, how are you going?" BJ asked the next day.

"Getting buggered. I'll be glad for this muster to end," she replied.

"Can we talk tonight, please … away from the others?" BJ asked, and Lizzy replied yes. Then out of nowhere they heard Kevin's voice. "BJ get back to work, NOW, you lazy son of a bitch!" He knew then that Kevin didn't want him around Lizzy.

And work they did, all day long. In the heat and the dust and the flies.

That night BJ and Lizzy moved away from the campfire so they could talk.

"How are you going, BJ?" Lizzy asked him.

"I'm going okay, actually loving it … I wanted to talk to you tonight while I have the guts to." BJ paused briefly, took a deep breath and then went on, "I've started to have feelings for you, Lizzy. This is new for me, but I have to tell you how I feel about you. I know at the moment we are all working hard at it and I have a job to do for your dad, so it's not the best time for this …"

"I've missed sitting around the campfire with you, and I have feelings for you too, BJ. I know we're heading back to the main house for a few days at the end of the week, so why don't we meet up at home?" Lizzy suggested.

"Yes, that would be great. Okay if I give you a hug goodbye?" he asked.

"Yes, I would love that," and she put her arms around BJ. Lizzy removed her hat and held it up so no one could see when they cuddled. As she embraced BJ she turned her head and gave him a kiss on the cheek. "Hey, I liked that," he whispered, and then he kissed her softly on her lips. Their first kiss. Lizzy kissed him back, softly at first and then with real desire. Neither wanted to stop, but BJ pulled away.

"I would love to keep going, but we have work tomorrow," he said reluctantly, and gave her a quick kiss. The feel of her slim body against his, the feel of her arms around him made him feels things he hadn't felt for a long time.

"Catch you later," they said to each other, and both headed to their swags. BJ didn't want the hug and the kiss to end, but he looked forward to the next time back at the main house.

What BJ and Lizzy didn't know was that Kevin had been watching them the whole time.

CHAPTER SEVEN

The next morning at breakfast Kevin was telling the blokes what they were going to be doing that day. For some strange reason BJ was put on camp duties which included looking after the poddy calves and collecting any new ones. All the blokes were complaining that it was Jim who gave out the jobs, not Kevin. Voices were raised and a few stood toe-to-toe with Kevin until Jim let out a loud whistle.

"Right, is someone going to bloody tell me what the fuck is going on? There is work to be done!" Jim yelled angrily.

Unbelievably, and unusually, the cook spoke up.

"Jim, this no good drongo, he is trying to tell everyone what jobs they're doing for the day. Funny part is that he said he and Lizzy would be overseeing the drafting. All the blokes know what to do, but this drongo comes in here and tries to tell everyone what to do. I take orders from you — not this idiot."

Kevin went to say something to the cook, but Jim

stepped in, "You will take orders from me, so shut the fucking hell up!" Kevin glared and Jim walked towards him and stood right next to him.

"You blokes — oh, and Lizzy — have been working so hard that at the end of the week we are heading back to the main house for three or four days. Like all of you I'm going to enjoy a shower and a bed," he told all the workers before adding, "now, out and do your work. BJ can you hold back for a minute? Just wait outside, mate."

Jim turned to Kevin, "Right, where do you bloody think you are going? You stay there. Are you the boss? NO. Are you in charge? NO. Who the fucking hell do you think you are?" Jim barked angrily while moving closer to Kevin, "Right, you mongrel, do you think I am blind and deaf? I've watched you for a while now. I don't know where you get off, but this is MY station, and the blokes work hard and know their jobs. I will not stand for some drongo idiot like you to come in and upset everything. OH, while I'm at it, you are to stay the fucking hell away from my daughter!"

By now Jim was face-to-face with Kevin. He was so mad that as he was yelling he was poking his finger into Kevin's chest with some force. "I know what you told the blokes, and it will be a cold day in hell before you will own this station. Now get the fuck out there and work. OH, and you're on a warning, as they call it these days. I won't stand for arseholes like you!" Kevin looked astonished, he certainly wasn't expecting Jim to roar at him like that.

BJ was a distance away from Jim and Kevin, but he could hear everything. Kevin walked past BJ and gave him a really dirty look and spat on the ground. BJ thought, *Fuck you, idiot!* and his next thought was, *Oh boy, what did Jim want? He didn't sound happy.* BJ took a big breath when Jim came walking towards him.

"Sorry about that, BJ. How are you going? Fitting in with the blokes okay?" Jim asked. "Oh … I've noticed you and Lizzy aren't spending as much time talking now… everything okay, mate?"

"I'm going well, a bit tired, but other than that loving the job. You're right, Lizzy and I haven't had much time to talk, but we have work to do and at the end of the day we're all buggered," BJ answered him.

They both got on their horses to head over to the yards when Jim said, "I'm not blind or silly. Sue and I picked up about you and Lizzy from the start. I've seen Kevin push his way in, and now I know he's trying to push you out. Hang in there, okay mate?"

BJ thanked Jim and headed over to where he would be working.

At last, and with much happiness it was the end of the week. Jim repeated what he had said days earlier, "We're heading back to the main house for three or four days." Everyone was happy about that and looking forward to being back at the main house.

When they reached the main house, the horses had to be looked after first, then the utes unloaded, and then it was a few days of free time. Time for a shower, do the washing, and get ready to head back out. Certain workers had to check over the trucks and machinery before they headed back out to the muster. Lizzy checked over the horses to make sure they were fine.

Kevin asked one of the female labourers, who only worked around the main house, to do his washing. This was met with a strong 'No', and in the end he did it, but much to his disgust. That night he went to the cookhouse for dinner. He was met with silence, and blokes turned away from him, moved away from him, and didn't talk to him. Some even spat on the ground near him. Was he happy? NO. After his meal he went in search of Lizzy.

"What the hell is he doing here?" Jim commented to Sue.

"I'm wondering if I can speak to Lizzy please?" he asked, and as he spoke she came to the door.

"Hi! Can we go for a walk please?"

They headed over to a big mango tree in the yard and stood under it. There was a little bit of light there as they were on the outer edge of the lights from the house and cookhouse.

"Lizzy, I've fallen for you, and I want to take it further," Kevin said.

Lizzy's alarm bells went off. *Christ! Who the hell is this bloke?*

"Now you can stop right there. I *don't* have feelings for you, I don't even like you," Lizzy stated. "I know what you said to the blokes, and no way would I marry an idiot, drongo, wanker, like you." She turned to walk off. He reached out and grabbed her arm and pulled her towards him. "It's in your best interest to let me go now!" she screamed. With that Jim was on the verandah and all the blokes were out of the cookhouse. Things went from bad to worse and when BJ did move, he was sprinting towards Lizzy.

Now Kevin was pushing Lizzy forcefully back against the tree trunk saying, "Lizzy, I love you." He was trying to kiss her and all the while she was fighting to get away. In his attempts to kiss her Kevin tore her shirt.

"Mate, back off now!" BJ said, full of anger as he reached the mango tree.

"Go away, Lizzy is mine not yours," Kevin said as he tried to kiss Lizzy again. By now Jim and the other workers were not far away.

It happened so quicky, but it felt like it was in slow-motion, BJ grabbed Kevin's shoulder and turned him around. With Kevin facing him, BJ let fly with a bunch of fives that knocked him to the ground. Kevin went to get up all the while saying words which BJ didn't hear.

And then the second punch to the jaw put Kevin out for the count.

BJ took off his shirt and put it on Lizzy. She was crying and lowered her head. He helped Lizzy back to the house, walking past all the other blokes and Jim. Sue ran down towards them and she bundled Lizzy into the house. BJ returned to Jim and the men.

"Get up, you dog!" was all Jim said to Kevin. As Kevin stood up he was gabbling that he was going to ring the police and have BJ charged. BJ couldn't help it, this was not really him, but he let loose with another bunch of fives. Jim pulled him off Kevin. "No one treats a woman like that!" BJ shouted at Kevin.

Jim squared up to Kevin, "Right, you are not going to ring the police. If you do, Lizzy will be ringing them to put a charge on you. Oh, don't worry I have a good solicitor so the charges would be many, and there are many witnesses. You'll never work on another station after this." All the workers had moved closer and they stood beside Jim.

Kevin pointed to BJ, "He assaulted me." Jim asked the workers, "Did any of you see BJ touch Kevin?" A resounding 'NO' was said by them all.

"Get the fuck off my station! Fuck off, you dog! Be warned that if you go to the police we will lay charges against you," Jim told Kevin.

Hearing all the noise, Harry, the station manager arrived. "Everything alright, Jim?" he asked.

"Harry, can you see this dog off the station? He has one hour. Any problems, come and get me."

Harry got hold of Kevin's arm and headed him towards the small house where he had been staying. Jim knew that Harry would handle the situation.

"You alright, BJ?" Jim asked.

"What the hell have I done? I'm on that stupid bond and if he goes to the cops I'm inside for years," BJ said trying to remain calm, but he sounded worried.

"Up to the house, come on, son," Jim ordered.

"Mum, can you get a us a beer please, and the first aid kit," Jim asked Sue.

"Son, you don't have to worry, it will be fine. Give me a look at your hand." Jim checked BJ's hands, "A bit of skin off, but I daresay you've had worse."

"Sue, how is Lizzy, is she okay?" Jim couldn't hide the concern in his voice.

"She's shaken up, but she'll be out in a moment, she's having a shower," Sue replied calmly.

While Jim and BJ were drinking their beer, Lizzy entered the kitchen.

"Thanks for your help, BJ," she said while handing him his shirt back.

"Are you alright, Lizzy? He didn't hurt you, did he?" asked BJ.

"No, he didn't," Lizzy answered and then, to

everyone's surprise, she put her arms around BJ. He stood up and cuddled her. She put her head on his shoulder and tears started to flow.

"Lizzy, you're okay, I'm here," he reassured her while holding her tightly.

This shocked Sue and Jim, they couldn't believe what they had just seen. BJ stayed with Lizzy until she said she was tired.

"Are you alright to head to bed?" he asked. She shook her head. BJ called out to Sue, " Sue, can you come here please?"

"Lizzy is tired and said she wants to go to bed. Can you help her please?" he asked. With a hand on his arm Sue said, "BJ, you help her, its alright. Lizzy, you show him where your room is."

BJ gave Sue a worried look and asked if she was sure. She nodded her head. Lizzy showed BJ to her room.

"I will just go and get into my pj's," she said. When she came back from the bathroom BJ had turned down the bedcovers for her. Lizzy got into bed and he pulled the covers over her. He gave her a kiss on the check and said he would see her in the morning.

"Lizzy is in bed now." BJ assured Sue and Jim when he returned to the kitchen. "Why has Kevin's behaviour affected her like this?" BJ asked them. "She seems such a strong woman to me."

"Last year a bloke tried something on with her and it

didn't end well. Remember, I said she took days to settle down? Well, I think tonight has brought all of that back for her. I think she will be fine," Jim explained.

BJ said goodnight to the two of them and went to the cookhouse for a coffee before heading to his cabin. He thought, *What a night!* It reminded him of what had happened to Bree. In the morning, he would talk to Lizzy again about what happened to Bree, and he would remind her about how she pulled through something similar. Anyway time for sleep. Sleep—all he could do was think about Lizzy, about what had happened, and it replayed over and over in his head. He was worried about Lizzy and hoped she was going to be alright.

Before going to sleep BJ thought long and hard. Lizzy was so much like Bree. Even though they hadn't known each other for very long he had made up his mind that, when the time was right, he was going to ask Lizzy to marry him. But first he had to talk to Jim and Sue.

After BJ had left Jim and Sue, they were still enjoying a beer when Harry knocked on the door.

"Jim, just letting you know that dog is off the property. I made sure he was all the way over the other side of the river," he said with a laugh, before adding, "Don't think he will get far though, he didn't have that much petrol in his flash car and I wouldn't let him buy any fuel from the station so he could fill up his tanks." This made all three of them laugh.

CHAPTER EIGHT

The next morning at breakfast Jim arrived at the cookhouse. "Morning everyone, after last night's incident with Kevin, I wanted to find out how everyone is." The men all nodded at Jim to show him they were okay. "As you all know, Kevin has been kicked off the station, so if anyone sees him, get onto me straight away. If he goes to the cops none of you are to talk to them, they talk to me. Got it? BJ, how are you today? How's the hand?"

"Morning, Jim, the hand's a bit sore, but it's okay," he answered. "Is Lizzy alright?"

All the blokes wanted to know how Lizzy was, and Jim told them she was okay, a bit shaken up, but she would be fine.

After breakfast BJ went over to the main house. "Morning, Sue, is Lizzy up yet?"

"Morning, BJ, yes she's up," and then Sue called out for Lizzy to come to the kitchen.

"Morning, Lizzy, how are you going? BJ asked her.

"Been better, but I will get there," she replied while giving BJ a quick cuddle.

"Can we sit down?" BJ asked, and they sat on the stools around the large kitchen bench. Looking at her and holding her hand, "Lizzy, when Bree had the run-in with the drunken idiots, it turned out that one of them had a father who was a crooked solicitor in a town close to Chilly. He came to Bree's house to bully her into dropping the charges made against his son. He was really abusive, and he even offered her money." BJ paused to make sure that Lizzy was taking it all in.

"Anyway, after she spoke to him she came back inside the house, and she collapsed and cried so much that Cody's dad called the doctor out to see her. She got help from a psychologist, and she's doing okay now, but it still took her a while to get over it. Lizzy, if you want to talk about anything I'm here. Remember, Kevin can never hurt you again. No one can, okay?" Lizzy gave BJ a hug and thanked him for reassuring her.

"Right, I have to get to work, you look after yourself today, and I'll call over tonight and catch up with you then," he said, smiling.

BJ called over that night to check on Lizzy, and even though she said she was doing fine, he was still concerned.

It was now August, everyone was back mustering, and

the cook had set up the camp again. At night BJ would sit with Lizzy around the campfire and they would talk. After the 'Kevin' episode BJ was watching Lizzy closely.

One day in the yards, BJ was helping sort out some of the cattle, and he was not on horseback. He had jumped on the rails a few times because of one bull in particular. Jim had already warned him that this bull was a mean bastard. A few of the blokes came over to help BJ push the bull into the race to get it onto the truck. A race is a fenced corridor that separates cattle from the rest of the herd. Everyone was up on the rails a few times, but this bull wasn't going to go into the race.

BJ saw Lizzy enter the yard. "Lizzy, out please! This bull is one mad shit, and I don't want you getting hurt." In that moment they both grabbed the top yard rail and quickly climbed up out of the way.

This bull was a crazy bastard.

"As the vet, what would you do with this bull?" BJ asked.

Lizzy answered that there was nothing she could do, she didn't have any tranquilisers close at hand.

"Please stay out of the yard, Lizzy, I don't want you to get hurt." BJ repeated, his concern obvious.

Jim came over and told Lizzy not to go into the yard. Like BJ, he didn't want to see her hurt either.

After a lot of yelling and locking gates behind the bull, it finally went into the truck. The truck, or rather the road train, had a load of cattle and it was heading to Stuart for the cattle sale in a few days. In the outback trucks that transport cattle mainly consist of a prime mover and three to four trailers, and many are double-deckers.

After the day spent loading the bulls all the blokes were buggered and were looking forward to dinner. The cook always had a good meal waiting for them. Jim always took his satellite phone with him on the muster, and would ring Sue after dinner.

"Hi, Sue, how's things there?" asked Jim.

"Everything's okay but, Cody, BJ's friend from down south rang at lunchtime. Unfortunately, I have bad news for him," she replied.

"Oh no, what's happened? Do you want me to get BJ?" Jim asked, his voice full of concern.

"No, can you please tell him? Unfortunately Paul passed away last night from a massive stroke. I told Cody I would pass the message on to BJ as he was out on a muster. Cody said to tell him don't come home, Paul would have wanted him to stay at work. What do you think about BJ giving Cody a ring on the sat phone?"

Jim said he would go and talk to BJ to suggest that he phoned Cody. "Thanks, Sue, I'll call again tomorrow night as usual."

Jim went in search of BJ and found him and Lizzy sitting around the campfire with the other blokes.

Jim called out to them, "Hey, BJ, can you and Lizzy meet me at the shed please?"

"Yep, no worries, Jim," BJ answered. The shed, which was built long ago, functioned as the cookhouse.

BJ and Lizzy arrived and sat on one of the benches in front of Jim. "Son, I have some bad news for you. I'm sorry to have to tell you this. Cody rang Sue at lunchtime today … unfortunately Paul passed away last night from a massive stroke. Cody said you should stay up here mustering as it is what Paul would have wanted." Jim could see how upset BJ had become. He had taken his hat off and bowed his head. Lizzy had one arm around him and she was holding his hand.

"You can ring Cody on the sat phone and talk to him, if you like," Jim suggested.

"Thanks, Jim, I would like to ring him. Lizzy, can you stay with me?" Jim stepped outside to give BJ some space.

BJ rang Cody's number. "Hi, Cody, I just got the sad news. How are Beth and Bree holding up?" he asked.

"Hi, mate, they're a mess, but Dad is here with me and we're organising everything. It was a huge shock to us all." Cody explained, "We took Paul to the pub for dinner and as we were leaving he collapsed on the footpath right outside the front door. The doctors said he would have died instantly as it was a massive stroke."

"When is his funeral, mate?" BJ asked. "I'll see if I can get home for it."

"No, mate, Paul would have wanted you to keep working … you know what he was like. Mate, stay up there, I know it must be a shock—are you okay?" Cody asked him.

"Yes, it's a bloody shock, wish I could make it home though. We're on a big muster in the middle of nowhere. Please give Bree and Beth a hug for me and let them know I'm doing alright and I wish I was there for you all," BJ said.

"No worries, mate, I'll do that. You look after yourself up there," Cody said.

"Okay, mate, I'll catch you later, love to everyone," and BJ ended the phone call.

He turned to Lizzy and hugged her tight and the tears came. Lizzy was hugging BJ back saying, "I'm here, it's going to be alright."

Jim walked back in and sat next to BJ. "You okay, son? I know it must be a blow for you. What was Paul like?"

BJ told Jim and Lizzy about Paul, his care for all of Bree's mates, how he couldn't work the farm anymore, and of the love between him and Beth.

BJ started to laugh, and Jim asked what was so funny. "The last thing Paul asked me when I said goodbye to everyone at the pub before coming up was, *'Well, are you going to bring home a wife from up there?'"*

Even Jim had a laugh at that. BJ's and Lizzy's eyes met. It was enough — they didn't have to say anything.

Jim offered to BJ that if he wanted to go home he would organise it, but BJ said no, he would honour Paul by working.

They talked a little longer and BJ fondly remembered Paul. After that BJ and Lizzy left Jim at the cookhouse and moved outside to the edge of the campfire's light. BJ had another cry while Lizzy hugged him. When he had finished he thanked Lizzy for her hugs and understanding.

"I'm here whenever you need a hug, or anything else. Always," she said.

"Always?" BJ asked. She nodded her head and leant into him, and they kissed each other just as the light from the full moon streamed down on them.

Considering everything that had happened on the station, what BJ had been through personally, and how understanding Jim and Sue had been through all of it, BJ decided it was time for a chat with Jim.

The next morning after breakfast as they were riding out, BJ caught up with Jim, "Hi, Jim, wondering if we can have a chat away from everyone's ears?"

"Yep. Everything okay, BJ?" Jim asked wondering what was wrong.

They dismounted from their horses and leant up against the steel railing of the yards where there were no workers to listen in.

"Jim, you and Sue have been really welcoming and understanding, and I appreciate that you took a chance on me for this job. This may come out wrong, and I apologise if it does. I know Sue is not here, but I want to do the right thing and ask you both if I have your blessing to ask Lizzy to marry me. I understand we haven't known each other long, but it feels like we have. I don't want an answer now, I want you to talk to Sue about it. I know we won't be back at the main house for about another week or two so there's no rush," BJ said. He thought to himself, *'Where did all those words come from? I've never been a talker like that!'*

"Sue and I guessed a while ago there was something between you and Lizzy, but we chose not to say anything. Lizzy is her own woman, and if she wants you that's okay with us. I'm amazed you've come to me and asked for Lizzy's hand in marriage. These days blokes don't often do that, but it shows that you have respect for me and Sue. I'll talk to her to see what she has to say, and let's say I will give you an answer when we get back to the main house. Now, if you do ask Lizzy do you have an engagement ring?" Jim said.

"Down home I have, a family heirloom," BJ replied.

"Right. Thanks for asking for our blessing, we better get back to work. Oh, and maybe you should move out of the light of the campfire at night. A couple of the blokes are watching you," Jim said, and with that they both got back to work.

CHAPTER NINE

The days wore on and the cattle came into the yards in big mobs. Some were quiet while others were wild.

At night BJ and Lizzy moved further out of the campfire's light, as they talked and laughed together.

One night, they were well out of the campfire light, and the tree canopy they were standing under allowed only partial moonlight to shine through. BJ was leaning up against an old gum tree and Lizzy was resting with her back against him while they chatted about all sorts of things. BJ looked up at the sky and remarked how clear it was and how bright the stars were.

Lizzy turned to face BJ and kissed him, and then kissed him some more. The kisses became more passionate, the hugs more sensual. The kisses on the neck became more intense, Lizzy licked BJ's ear and even the taste of dust did not stop her from letting her tongue travel down his neck and around to his chest. BJ responded in the same way, giving in to the intensity of his feelings. He pulled Lizzy's shirt out from her jeans and as he kissed her he let his hands travel over her slim body.

Lizzy easily undid the press studs on BJ's shirt and ran her hands over his muscular chest. She felt his hands running over her breasts, gently cupping them. Lizzy wasn't wearing a bra and feeling her breasts in his hands stirred a desire BJ had not felt for a long time.

The night may have been cool, but the heat between them was hotter than a summer's day. Neither wanted to, but they had to stop as they knew where it was heading.

Lizzy told BJ that his whiskers tickled her.

"No time for shaving out here," he said while tucking his shirt back into his jeans.

Lizzy's hands travelled down the sides of BJ's face. "I love your moustache, but not your beard. When we get back to the main house you'll have to shave, but leave the moustache," she said.

"I've never had one, always been clean shaven. That's what I was taught, but out here shaving is not on the list for me. I know your dad does, but I'm happy to grow a beard and shave it off after the muster. I'll think about leaving a moustache," BJ said.

"And if I want you to have one?!" Lizzy said, still holding BJ's face in her hands.

"We will see … come here," he said.

BJ couldn't let Lizzy go without another cuddle and

more kisses, but their kisses again became so intense that they were both getting turned on.

"We better stop … as much as I would love to continue this," BJ said reluctantly.

They walked back into the light from the campfire and went their separate ways to their swags to get some sleep — if they could sleep, as they were both thinking about what *could* have happened.

The next morning, Thursday, everyone was up and heading to work. They all knew from previous years that they would be heading back to the main house either at the weekend or the following weekend. This muster had been a long and hard-working one.

The cattle that came in from the muster where wild, and there were many that went on the truck to go to sale. Many truck loads, or rather road trains, of cattle had come from the muster. All the jackaroos were counting down the days to the end of the muster, and BJ was really looking forward to hearing Jim's and Sue's answer to his request.

On Sunday morning at breakfast, Jim stood up.

"Fella's, thank you for all the hard work you have done on the muster. From talking to the chopper pilots and from all the mustering guys we will be finished mustering today. All that will be left is getting them through the yards and sorting them out. If we get the work done today we can head back to the main house tomorrow. Daresay you blokes are like me, would love a shower and a proper bed, and some of us need to find a razor. But everything has to be packed up in time, so it's up to all of you," announced Jim.

A chorus of voices rang out, "Let's go, let's finish this off,"… "I'm looking forward to a hot shower,"… "Christ, I'm looking forward to a few beers!" There was finger-pointing and laughter about the ones who needed a razor.

Jim urged them, "Let's go then. Cookie, can you start packing up while you're still feeding us all?"

"Bloody oath, I can pack it up. I'm looking forward to a few beers," Cookie said excitedly.

Lizzy hung back for BJ. "I can't wait to get home, and have a long hot shower to wash this dust off me."

"Oh, I wish I was there to wash that dust off you," BJ said, smiling and sneaking a kiss on Lizzy's neck.

"I don't think we would be doing much washing though," Lizzy said with a smile, and they both headed off to the yards.

Everyone got stuck in and the work was finished before they knew it. That night Cookie and a few of the blokes packed everything except what they needed for breakfast.

Jim had never seen so many men get in and do a job so quickly. He thought, *When we get home I'll put on a barbecue and let the guys have some beers, they've earned it.* Then he called Sue on the sat phone, "Evening, Sue, we're heading home tomorrow, so watch for the dust clouds. It'll be great to be home and even better to see you … and I can't wait for a shower."

"Oh, that's great, I've missed you too. This muster has been a long one," Sue replied.

"Oh, I have to talk to you about something as well. I don't want to say anything on the phone, but we have to sit down and have a talk," Jim said.

"No worries, I'll see you tomorrow."

The next morning everyone's gear was packed up and they had started loading everything on to the trucks. Cookie had made breakfast, and after everyone had finished eating they packed up the last of the items. Horses loaded, poddy calves loaded. Everywhere Jim looked everything was on the trucks ready to go. He had never seen a mustering camp packed up so quickly, even the fires had been put out properly. After one final check, they left the now-deserted camp and headed back to the main house.

BJ and Lizzy were in the truck with Jim and another two workers. They sat holding hands and leaning into each other. Lizzy fell asleep, and BJ put his arm around her shoulders and let her head rest on his chest. Jim saw this in the rear-view mirror and had a chuckle to himself.

After many hours of driving, bouncing in their seats and being thrown around on the rough roads, they arrived at the main house just before afternoon tea time. They hadn't stopped for lunch as they all wanted get home as soon as they could.

Sue had come out of the house as soon as she saw the dust clouds churned up by the trucks driving on the dry roads. Jim walked over to Sue, and in a surprise to her and to all the men, gave her a cuddle followed by a long kiss. Sue was taken aback by this. And Lizzy thought, *Hmm … that's a little strange, Dad doesn't normally show affection in front of the men.*

"Jim Gordon, into the shower, you are dusty and you stink! Oh, it looks like a few of you need razors. I have plenty at the main house if you need them," Sue laughed.

Trucks were unloaded, horses were attended to, and gear was stowed in their cabins. Thankfully Sue had turned on the air conditioning in everyone's cabin.

As the horses were unloaded, Lizzy completed a full vet check over each one. She was pleased to confirm that all the horses were fine.

Jim walked hand-in-hand with Sue over to the main house. Like most of the men, the first thing he did after the unloading was done was have a shower.

While BJ was having his shower, he couldn't get the thought of Lizzy naked in her shower out of his mind. After showering, it was time for a shave, he thought, *I've never had a moustache … oh well, have a shave, leave the moustache, and see what it looks like.* BJ shaved his beard and chin and tidied up around the moustache.

He looked in the mirror and thought, *Not bad, and it's easy enough to take off later if I decide I don't like it.*

That night at dinner, all the blokes looked cleaner, and most were clean shaved. They all agreed the first shower after a muster was great!

CHAPTER TEN

The next morning everyone was a bit late rising because the beds were so comfortable after the swags, the flies, and the heat. BJ was first to get up and went for a coffee at the cookhouse.

"Morning, Cookie, how are you going today? I'm just in for a coffee," BJ said.

"Morning, BJ, I'm okay. I didn't want to get up out of the bed though, it felt so good to sleep in and I slept like a baby," Cookie replied. "I just made the coffee so it's nice and hot. What's this? A new look, a moustache?"

"They say a change is as good as a holiday, don't they? Easy to shave off if I don't like it."

"I think there is one lady that will love it," Cookie remarked with a wide grin.

"Cookie, what are you on about?" BJ said with an embarrassed laugh. To change the conversation BJ asked, "Everyone still asleep I take it?"

"No, Jim is up and he's been doing the rounds checking on everything," Cookie said with a grin.

"What's so funny?" BJ asked him.

"You don't know Jim yet, but there's no stopping that bloke, here or on a muster he is go, go, go. I can see what Sue means when she says she wants him to slow down," Cookie replied thoughtfully.

Jim walked into the cookhouse and his ears must have been ringing from Cookie and BJ talking about him. "Morning, fellas, how are you?" he asked, while pouring a coffee. Both Cookie and BJ replied, "We're good thanks, Jim."

"Did you enjoy sleeping in your own beds? … BJ, what the hell? You forget to shave your upper lip?" Jim asked.

"Yep," BJ and Cookie both answered. BJ grinned and poured another coffee.

One by one the other workers came into the cookhouse, some looking a bit worse for wear. Not so much from drinking, but from trying to catch up on much-needed sleep that would need more than one night to fix. A few commented to BJ about his new moustache, but it was all in good fun.

"Lizzy up, Jim?" BJ asked.

"Yep, she is over with the horses, she's just keeping an eye on them after the muster," replied Jim.

"I'll go over and give her a hand," BJ said, and he headed to the stables.

"Morning, Lizzy, how are you going?" he asked.

Lizzy replied she was fine and that she was giving the horses another going over, just to be certain they had no issues from being on the muster.

"Everything okay so far?" BJ enquired.

"A few have needed their hooves cleaned out, but otherwise they're good."

When she had finished the last horse she stood up and looked at BJ. "Wow, I love the moustache! Makes you look even more sexy than you are," Lizzy said as she walked towards BJ and gave him a hug. "I thought of you when I was having my shower last night. I can't stop thinking about what we might have done," she said.

BJ smiled, he looked to see if anyone was around and grabbed Lizzy's hand. He took her into one of the stalls. "I thought we would be like this," and he started kissing her neck and pulling her shirt out of her jeans and letting his hands wander over her body. He went to grab the button of her jeans, but stopped himself. He knew it wasn't the place to continue where they had left off. As much as he wanted to keep going, he knew it wasn't right, and they hadn't discussed having sex yet. Still, he was so turned on by her that the heat in the stall was like being in a sauna.

All the while Lizzy had been responding to his touch. BJ's shirt was undone and out of his jeans. She had been kissing his neck and chest, but she stopped too when BJ did.

"Hmm … I think we better stop here," she said with a nervous laugh as she dressed.

"Yep, but we have to talk about something though," BJ said while buttoning his shirt and tucking it back into his jeans, even though what he really wanted to do was lay Lizzy down on the floor of the stall and kiss every inch of her body … run his hands over her soft skin … feel the arousal between her legs. But then he caught himself, *Come on mate, think of something else …*

They were both dressed now and smiled at each other as they both took a deep breath. They headed over to the round yard, and as no other workers were around, BJ asked Lizzy a question.

"We're starting to really get hot and steamy now. What's your thought on … hmm … taking it … " before BJ could finish the sentence Lizzy interrupted him. "For the love of God, BJ, just plain ask me what you want!"

BJ looked around and saw no one so he took Lizzy into his arms and gazed into her beautiful eyes, "I've got a feeling we both want the same thing. I want to lay you down and make passionate love to you, and I'm guessing that you feel the same."

Lizzy grinned, "Well, that's straight to the point. Yes, I want to make wild, passionate love to you as well."

BJ sighed, "We don't have a place with any privacy for that at the moment, so we're going to have to be careful. As much as I would love to lay you down in that horse stall and kiss you all over and for both of us to experience orgasm after orgasm all night long we're going to have to be careful," BJ said.

Lizzy leant into him and kissed his neck, "I would love you to lay me down and kiss me all over, and I can't wait to feel you inside me and … "

Lizzy stopped, she pulled back from BJ and took a deep breath. Then she added cheekily, "Love the moustache, don't shave it off."

They separated then, but still held hands while they walked back to the cookhouse. Sue spotted them walking over and called for Jim.

"Come here, Jim, quickly!"

Jim was next to her in a flash. "What's wrong, are you alright?"

While pointing in the direction of Lizzy and BJ, Sue announced, "Well, have a look at that, looks like we were right."

"Can you grab us a coffee and meet me on the verandah, please? We have to talk," Jim said.

Seeing BJ and Lizzy walking together hand-in-hand Jim knew he had to talk to Sue, he couldn't put it off any longer.

"What's wrong, Jim? This sounds serious," Sue said as she returned with the two coffees.

"Out on the muster—after Kevin pulled his shit—BJ

asked to talk to me. Believe it or not that bloke has respect for us both. He asked me for Lizzy's hand in marriage but wanted me to talk to you and to give him an answer once we had spoken," Jim said.

"Ahh … that hits the nail on the head. Lizzy came to me before the muster and asked how we knew we loved each other, and how we knew we were right for one another. I can see how much BJ loves Lizzy, and he really cares about her. I don't have any worries other than he doesn't have a lot of money. But really that's nothing when he's such a hard worker and Lizzy is a vet. Anyway, look at us—we didn't have a penny to our name," Sue supposed. Then she asked Jim, "Does BJ have an engagement ring?"

"Christ, you can talk the leg of one of Cookie's iron pots. Is it yes or no?" Jim asked, grinning.

"It's a yes from me, what do you say?" Sue said.

"I'm both ways, I know Lizzy is happy with BJ, but she is still my little my girl," Jim said.

"Jim Gordon, for the love of God, she is twenty-five years old. She will always be your girl, but she's an adult now. Oh, you sometimes make me so mad. I say yes to the proposal, what do you say? I want an answer!" Sue was standing in front of Jim with her hands on her hips leaning towards him.

"Yes, I agree to the proposal. I better find BJ and talk to him. At least this will put him out of his misery wondering what we've decided," Jim said while getting up out of his chair.

"Thanks, Sue, now don't you say anything to Lizzy," he said as he gave Sue a kiss.

Jim went in search of BJ and found him at the cookhouse.

"BJ, can you come with me please?" Jim showed no emotion in his voice—he was not giving anything away.

They headed over to the house. "Hi Sue, everything okay? Jim, you have me worried," BJ said.

"Mum, you do the talking and I will keep an eye out," Jim said.

"Jim has spoken to me about what you said to him on the muster. We guessed there was something between you two from the beginning. We both give you our blessing to marry Lizzy. Jim said you have an engagement ring down south, and that it's an heirloom," Sue said.

BJ got off the stool and hugged Sue, "Thank you, both of you. You have made my day. Yes, the ring I have at home is my great, great grandma's, but it will probably need some repairs and some resetting and remodelling. So, I have decided to buy a new ring for Lizzy. I was hoping you could help me with that, Sue. You know Lizzy's taste and her ring size."

"Yes, of course I will help you BJ. You do one thing for me though: you look after our girl, and if you ever need anything, we are here. Do you know when you will ask Lizzy to marry you?" asked Sue.

 "I don't know when yet, I wanted to get your permission before I thought about anything else. I really appreciate the help, Sue."

BJ went over to Jim and put out his hand, Jim took his hand and shook it firmly then he slapped BJ on the back. "Look after my girl," Jim said.

 "Of course, Jim, I will," BJ left the house and went to his cabin to check emails and sort his washing.

CHAPTER ELEVEN

Three days later Sue knocked on BJ's cabin door. "Come in, Sue, what have you got there?" he asked.

"I have a printout of engagement rings, for you to look at," Sue said, grinning.

"What's funny, Sue?" BJ wondered what was up.

"Last night Lizzy caught me looking online at engagement rings. I emailed the jeweller in town, and he sent me through a catalogue. Question after question, and in the end she was sitting with me looking at them. I told her our cousin was getting engaged, but as he works in the mines and can't get into town he had asked for my help," Sue gave a laugh.

"Boy, that was close! So, all these rings are the ones Lizzy picked out, is that right?" BJ asked.

They sat at the table and Sue explained the details of each ring while she and BJ looked closely at each picture. Finally, they reached the last ring. It was a simple design with a central solitaire diamond, surrounded by smaller diamonds, all within a traditional setting.

"Did Lizzy like this one?" BJ asked.

"Funny you should say that, because this was her favourite. Which ones do you like?"

"Me … I like numbers two and four and seven. But if Lizzy loves number seven then that's the one I will go for," BJ decided. "Just wondering if the jeweller in town has them in stock or do they make them to order? Did you find out Lizzy's ring size?"

"Yes to the size, and yes the jeweller in town has it in stock. All I have to do is call him and he will put the right one aside until it can be collected," explained Sue.

"I'll organise a day, with Jim's permission, when I can go into town to pick it up," BJ said.

"You don't have to worry about that, BJ. I have to go into town in a few days and I can pick it up for you then, and I'll keep it in the safe at the main house." Sue had really thought this through. "You can transfer the money to my personal bank account, not the business account you get paid from."

"Hang on a minute. Do you know the details of your bank account?" asked BJ. "I can transfer the money to you now."

Sue pulled out a piece of paper from her pocket with the information he needed and she handed it to BJ. She was amazed when she saw BJ transfer the amount for the ring and a bit more.

"Sue, thanks a lot for helping me with this. Could you please make sure the ring is exactly what I ordered when you pick it up, and please pick up something for yourself at the same time. I've transferred the cost of the ring and another five hundred dollars for you," BJ said.

"Son, you don't have to do that, it's my honour to help you. I'll make sure the ring is perfect, and it will be hidden safely until you ask for it," Sue said while getting up off the chair.

"Thanks, Sue, I better find some work to do. I don't like being bored," BJ admitted. She reached up and gave him a warm hug and then left his cabin.

He thought to himself, *Now, when and where do I ask Lizzy to marry me?* First though, it was back to work, and he left his cabin to go and find something useful to do.

The next morning at breakfast, Jim arrived and spoke to everyone at the cookhouse.

"Okay, everyone, quiet please! I know the last muster was a big one, but we have one more this year. In a week's time we leave for a short two-week muster.

"Old Jimmie, you know the camp called *Bull's Head?*" Old Jimmie nodded. "Well, that's where we're going. According to the workers who are mending fences in the area there's a lot of wild cattle there. This time we're taking motorbikes and horses. The chopper guys will help us, but we have to be bloody careful." Everyone was paying close attention, so Jim continued, "The fence guys said the cattle are 'bloody crazy'. As some of you would know, Bull's Head is a rough camp so enjoy your bed and your shower while you can. Water will be on one of the trucks, but it's drinking water only. For everything else there's a water trough. BJ, as you are fairly new to mustering here, you can stay put and work on the property for this one."

BJ responded, "Thanks for the offer, Jim, but you employed me as a jackaroo, and I'll be on the muster with everyone else." He didn't want any special treatment. Bull's Head camp was closer to the main house than the other camps, but far enough away that the wild cattle didn't come anywhere near the main house.

"BJ, you're new at this, and these mongrels are really wild and dangerous," warned Wally. "You'll need eyes in the back of your head. If you need help with anything just ask me, okay mate."

"Thanks for the heads-up, Wally," and BJ touched his right side where he wore his pistol.

"That won't stop these wild mongrels, you'll need a bigger gun than that," Wally said.

"Thanks again for the advice, Wally, I better get going." BJ headed to his cabin to pick up a few things and then headed over to the sheds to help get everything ready.

On most nights BJ and Lizzy would meet up on the verandah of the main house or anywhere else that was quiet. That night BJ asked Lizzy if she had been to the Bull's Head camp before and if the cattle were as bad as everyone said they were.

"Yes, I've been there, and the cattle *are* crazy! You have to be careful," replied Lizzy.

The next morning after breakfast BJ ran into Jim. "Jim, you know I wear a pistol, but Wally said it would not be big enough for the cattle at Bull's Head. Well, I have a rifle and pouch for my saddle … would it be okay if I took my rifle on the muster?" BJ asked.

"Son, you can, but I still worry about you on this run," Jim said.

"Is Lizzy going on the muster? I'm more worried about her than me."

"Me too, but you can't talk her out of it," Jim said, shaking his head.

By now it was the second half of September, and the camp at Bull's Head was set up and running. Cookie had the kitchen all set up, and the trucks were unloaded of all goods and equipment. Jim had brought an electric fence to keep the wild cattle out of the camp and to keep the workers safe. Additionally, all the trucks and utes were parked in a rough circle around the camp, and the campfire was kept going night and day as a deterrent to the wild cattle.

Jim spoke to everyone at breakfast the next morning, "Well, you've already seen the danger we are dealing with. All the cattle will be going straight into the trucks for sale. From now on, I want you working in groups of three for safety reasons. The chopper will round up the cattle further out and push them closer. But everyone keep your eyes out and watch each other, and if anything happens jump on the UHF radio straight away. Let's get out there and get them. Lizzy, BJ, and Noel, hold on a moment please."

The three of them stayed back and Jim spoke directly to them, "You three are to ride together at all times, and be very careful out there. Make sure each of you has a UHF radio," Jim said firmly, hoping Lizzy would be safe. The three mounted their horses, and Noel rode slightly ahead of the other two. BJ spoke quietly to Lizzy, "Lizzy, please be careful, I worry about you because I care about you."

This proved to be the wrong thing to say. "I may be a woman, but I have mustered for a long time," Lizzy snapped back at BJ and took off on her horse. BJ wondered what he'd done wrong, but he didn't have time to dwell on it. It was time to work so he rode on to catch up with the others.

CHAPTER TWELVE

It was now the last week in September and the day was frantic: mustering, getting out of the road of mad cattle, and on and on until late that afternoon.

Lizzy, Noel, and BJ were at the rear of a mob of cattle when suddenly a large bull turned to the right, instead of going forward, and headed off into the bush.

"Push them up, Noel!" yelled BJ. Lizzy raced off after the bull and BJ chased after Lizzy. When he caught up to them he saw Lizzy and then he saw the bull turn towards her. BJ could see what was going to happen and immediately he reached around for his rifle. The big bull hit Lizzy side on. Her horse went down, and Lizzy was thrown. BJ dropped Bingo's reins and with a perfect shot killed the bull. Then one-handed BJ let of a shot, then another, then another: three shots, a signal for help needed. Next, without even thinking about it he was screaming into the UHF radio, "Help! Help! Lizzy's been taken out by a bull. Help!"

He was riding towards Lizzy at breakneck speed, while screaming into the radio, "Jim, you on air?!

Help! Lizzy's been hit by a big bull. She's not moving! Grab my swag and the first-aid kit from camp—Noel knows which way we headed."

BJ jumped off Bingo and placed his rifle against a tree for safety. He ran to Lizzy and gently held her, but she was unresponsive. The chopper pilot had heard BJ's urgent call on the radio and now flew overhead guiding Jim where to go.

When BJ saw the dust cloud from the approaching ute he waved his hat to get Jim's attention. The ute skidded to a stop and Jim ran to Lizzy.

"Lizzy, can you hear me?!" Jim screamed. There was no response. Nothing. "Sue, you on air? Over!" Jim shouted desperately into the radio.

The radio crackled and he heard Sue say, "On air, Jim. Go ahead."

"We need the Flying Doctor, Lizzy has been hurt badly. She's unconscious!" Jim screamed into the radio.

"Okay, copy that," was all Sue said.

The pilot had landed the chopper as close as it was possible to where Lizzy lay, but it was still a short distance away. He ran over to them and was now beside BJ, Jim, and Noel.

BJ checked Lizzy's vital signs, she was breathing, but it was shallow and irregular; he felt her legs and he didn't like what he found. He was worried, "I need four strong branches to help splint Lizzy's legs," announced BJ.

"The first aid kit—I need the heavy bandages to tie the branches to the outside of Lizzy's legs to immobilise them. Can someone get me my swag?" BJ said in a strong, loud voice.

"BJ, what's wrong?" Jim asked.

"Noel, take over here please," BJ said to Noel, and he moved away to talk to Jim privately.

"Jim, I felt Lizzy's left leg and it feels broken, and she's not breathing normally so she may have internal injuries. I'm wondering if the chopper can fly Lizzy back to the airstrip to meet the Flying Doctor. We'll need something to slide under her to keep her steady until then," BJ said, while looking at Lizzy, his voice concerned.

Jim called the chopper pilot over to where he and BJ were talking. "Can you fly Lizzy back to the airstrip at the main house? Are you licensed to fly at night?" Jim grilled him.

"Yep, I can fly Lizzy back to the airstrip, and my licence is night-rated. This is an emergency, and the Flying Doctor can't land anywhere near here." The pilot continued, hoping to reassure Jim, "Luckily I'm flying the bigger chopper today instead of the smaller mustering one. There's room to slide Lizzy into the cabin and it's a doors-on helicopter."

"Wally, go back to camp and get the table. If you have to smash the legs off the bloody thing, do it. Also, tell the other blokes to get out here bloody quick smart. Go!" Jim ordered.

"Jim, do you copy?" Sue's voice came through the radio.

"Go ahead," he replied.

"The Flying Doctor will be here on the airstrip as soon as possible, but it could be a while because they're coming from another job on a remote property. Are you able to move Lizzy back to the airstrip at all? Over," Sue said.

"We're going to slide the tabletop under Lizzy and put her in the back of the ute, and drive to the chopper. The chopper pilot said he can fly Lizzy back to the northern end of the airstrip to meet the Flying Doctor there and BJ will go in the chopper with her. The chopper pilot says his ETA is around 7 pm—getting close to dark. Out."

Jim was really worried about his girl. Why was she so bloody stubborn?! He was hoping she would make it. Everything was happening at once: a couple of blokes came back with tree branches they had cut for splints, then Wally returned with all the other blokes, and the tabletop, and more.

BJ took control and gave everyone their orders. Old Jimmie had checked out the bull and confirmed it was dead, and he told Jim that Lizzy's horse was dead too, killed by the bull when it charged her.

"Okay everyone, I want to slide the tabletop under Lizzy, you have to watch you don't move her legs and her back. I prefer no movement at all," directed BJ.

"Hold on, I'll dig some of the sand out so you can start to slide the table under her," Frank said.

BJ asked for someone to back the ute up closer to where they were so it would be easier to slide the tabletop on to it.

"Alright, everyone ready?" BJ asked. "Lift on my call: one … two… three … lift!"

It went perfectly, now they had to get the tabletop up on to the tray of the ute. With four blokes each side they shuffled to the back of the ute and very gently slid the table onto the tray. BJ gently climbed up there beside Lizzy, who was still unresponsive.

"Jim, will you drive the ute? I'll sit back here with Lizzy. Noel, do you want to climb up here with me?" BJ was firing orders in every direction, "Frank, can you look after the horses and grab Lizzy's gear off her horse? Wally, can you go to the camp and grab my gear and meet us at the airstrip?"

Jim drove as smoothly as he could over the rough ground to the chopper, BJ took off his hat and held it up over Lizzy's face to keep the dust and the flies off her. He didn't show it, but he was anxious for her and inside he was a mess.

After driving for what seemed like ages, they reached the chopper, and carefully slid the tabletop with Lizzy on it into the cabin.

"I won't take my eyes off Lizzy, I'll look after her, Jim," BJ shouted over the sound of the chopper's rotors. He gently placed the earmuffs over Lizzy's ears, leaving the headband piece to sit below her chin, keeping her head as still as possible. He closed the door, and then jumped into the back seat so he could keep an eye on Lizzy.

The pilot radioed back to base and updated them on what had happened and where he was going next. He requested an emergency flight plan and lifted off as soon as it was granted. He flew the chopper low, but high enough to clear the trees. It seemed ages before the airstrip lights came into view. Thankfully, Sue had arranged for one of the workers to turn on the airstrip lights and the lights around the immediate area. The chopper landed safely, and shortly after the engine had shut down, Jim and a few of the other blokes arrived at the airstrip just as the hum of the Flying Doctor's plane could be heard above. BJ checked Lizzy to see how she was. No change.

The plane taxied to the end of the airstrip and a doctor and nurse jumped out. Jim introduced BJ and the doctor asked a string of questions. Then he spoke to Jim, "Jim, it feels like BJ was right, Lizzy may have leg fractures, and I'm worried that she's been unconscious for some time now. I think its best we head to Stuart

Hospital. There's only enough room for one of you to come with us." Jim nodded, then he turned to BJ.

"BJ, you got your wallet and phone?" BJ confirmed he did. "Alright, you go with Lizzy, and we'll meet you there later," Jim said.

"Jim … my rifle … can you get it and lock it up please? Here's the last of the ammunition I had on me. I'll stay in contact with you and I'll let you know how Lizzy is doing," BJ assured him. Jim gave BJ a bear-hug, much to the surprise of everyone there.

BJ jumped on the plane as instructed by the pilot. Jim radioed Sue back at the main house and updated her on everything that had happened, including that BJ was flying to the hospital with Lizzy.

When he ended the radio call Jim turned to the blokes at the airstrip and fired out orders. "Okay, all you guys go back to camp. Cookie, put the table on something to prop it up. Just have dinner, turn in for the night, and start again tomorrow. Wally, did you get BJ's rifle? Okay, Harry will be in charge while I'm away. All the cattle have to be trucked out for sale, and I'll stay in contact with Harry with updates on how Lizzy is doing."

"Jim, here's BJ's rifle … bloody nice rifle too!" Wally assured Jim, "We'll deal with Lizzy's horse and we'll look after her saddle and all her riding gear too."

Jim gave his final instructions to the men, "I'm going to the main house, and then Sue and I will head to

Stuart Hospital in my ute. I'll update Harry on the situation while I'm at the main house and he'll join you at the camp to help finish the job. Right, can someone run me up to the main house, please?"

The men all wished Jim their best for Lizzy and said they would be waiting for updates on her condition.

CHAPTER THIRTEEN

It was just after 7 pm when the Flying Doctor plane left the airstrip and headed to Stuart. When they landed at the Stuart airstrip later in the evening an ambulance was already waiting for them.

Sue had already contacted the hospital and given them all of Lizzy's details, including her medical information. The emergency doctor came and spoke to BJ and asked him what happened. As it had played over and over in his mind, BJ told the doctor exactly what he witnessed and what first aid he had given to Lizzy.

"Who put the splints on each side of Lizzy's legs?" the doctor asked.

"I felt her legs and it felt like she had a fracture on the left leg. So I got the blokes to cut some branches for splints, and with their help I tied heavy bandages around them to hold them in place. I was more worried about her breathing though … still am." replied BJ.

"Lizzy is having a CT scan now, and I will know more about her injuries after that. When will her parents arrive?" the doctor asked.

"They're on their way here, but it will take a couple hours' driving. Why?" BJ asked.

"You're not listed as family or next of kin."

"Hold on," BJ said, as he punched numbers into his phone. "Sue, the doctor is here with me, they bloody well won't tell me anything and they're asking me when you'll get here."

"Son, put your phone on speaker." BJ switched the audio to speakerphone and Sue spoke directly to the doctor, "Doctor whoever you are, I'm Lizzy Gordon's mother, Sue. I give my full permission for you to tell BJ everything and for him to act on our behalf until we get there. We're on our way. Do we have a problem now, doctor?" Sue screamed angrily into the phone.

"Thanks, Mrs Gordon, I'll keep BJ informed of everything that we find out regarding your daughter," the doctor said and then walked off.

"Christ, Sue! You laid down the law to that idiot. See you when you get here," BJ grinned.

"Stupid upstart! Wait until I get there, he's going to find out I'm not happy. How did Lizzy go on the plane?" Sue asked.

"She's still unconscious, the doctor seemed worried, but they won't know anything more until they finish the CT scan. I'll see you both when you get here," BJ said as he ended the call.

He asked a nurse who was nearby where he could get a coffee from.

"I'll get you one, how do you have it?" the young nurse asked. She returned with a mug of coffee and asked BJ, "Have you come straight from work?" BJ explained the events that lead to him being at the hospital, and after she returned to her duties he rang Cody.

"Hi mate," was all BJ could say before he started to cry.

"Mate, what's wrong? What's happened? BJ talk to me." Cody said, clearly worried.

BJ took a deep breath. "I'm at Stuart Hospital with Lizzy. We were mustering some wild cattle and she got taken out by a wild bull. Looks like she has a fractured leg and she's been unconscious for hours … I'm frightened I'm going to lose her," BJ sobbed through the tears.

"Mate, who is Lizzy?" Cody asked. BJ realised he had never told Cody about Lizzy and his feelings for her.

"Lizzy is the boss's daughter and I've fallen deeply in love with her. I haven't said anything before now because I didn't know where it was headed. I love her, Cody, and I haven't had the chance to tell her," BJ started to sob again. "I don't want to lose her, Cody. How did you cope when Bree had her accident?"

"Lizzy is in the best place. Yes, it's bloody hard. You feel useless. Bree didn't wake up for a day either, mate. Hang in there. Ring me later and let me know how you and Lizzy are going, okay," Cody said.

"How are you all doing down there?" BJ asked.

"Mate, we're doing alright, Beth has her good days. BJ, I know it's hard, but you *will* get through this. You can ring me anytime," Cody said in a caring voice. He knew exactly what BJ was going through after his own experience with Bree's accident near Dutchman's Road last year. How could he tell Bree any of this? She had done so well to recover from her accident, and he didn't want to drag it all up again. They talked for a while longer and BJ hung up just as the doctor returned.

"Hi BJ, we've completed the x-rays and CT scans, and you were right, Lizzy does have a fractured leg. The tibia and fibula of her left leg are fractured from the impact of the bull, however, her leg doesn't require surgery." The doctor paused to make sure BJ was following what he was explaining. "You were right to be concerned about her breathing, but she has nothing wrong there other than severe bruising over her body from when she was thrown from her horse. I believe she just had the wind knocked out of her, that's why her breathing was irregular. She has no other internal injuries. We're still concerned that she hasn't woken up, but her head scans are clear … we presume she hit her head when she was thrown. We've put her leg in a cast, so she won't be able to work or ride for about eight weeks. How big was the bull that hit her horse? You saw it happen, didn't you?" the doctor enquired.

"I saw the bull charging at Lizzy and her horse, and it hit her right on her left leg. The bull was big enough. Then I saw Lizzy and her horse hit the ground. The ground was sandy, not hard and dry … I don't know if that helps at all," BJ said.

"We're moving Lizzy to the Intensive Care Unit (ICU), so when she is settled someone will come and get you so you can be with her," the doctor said.

It was now about 10 pm, and BJ rang Sue to update her, "Hi Sue, the doctor has just spoken to me. Lizzy is very lucky to only have fractured her leg. She has bruising all over her body, and she's still unconscious. They're moving her to ICU. How far away are you and Jim?"

"BJ, Jim here, we're about an hour or so away." Sue had turned the phone audio to speaker. "When we get there we'll find you. Are you okay, son?"

"Still in shock, and I'm worried about Lizzy. I wish she hadn't insisted on going on the muster," BJ broke down started to cry. He walked outside and continued the phone call.

"Son, we will be there shortly … none of this is your fault," Jim reassured BJ, and ended the call.

BJ stood outside under a tree and had a good cry. His

thoughts turned to the angel who walked into the kitchen earlier in the year. The hugs, the kisses, the feel of Lizzy's skin … her smile. BJ knew Lizzy was the one he wanted to spend his life with, and he decided that he had to ask her to marry him sooner, rather than later.

The young nurse found him outside, "BJ, we've moved Lizzy to ICU, you can come and sit with her now."

"Thanks, can you show me the way please?"

The nurse saw that BJ had been crying and she asked if he was alright and if he would like another coffee. He said yes to both and told her that Lizzy's parents, Jim and Sue, were not far away.

When BJ saw Lizzy, his eyes filled with tears. He stopped at the end of the bed and looked at her.

Why can't that be me instead of Lizzy? BJ thought. He pulled a chair up alongside the left side of Lizzy's bed. He reached out and took her hand and kissed it.

Then the tears started again. The nurse came back with his coffee and saw that BJ was crying, "BJ, Lizzy is going to be okay, we just need her to wake up. Are you two a couple?" she asked.

"I love her so much and haven't even told her yet," he said as the tears slowed.

"When people are unconscious they can still hear you. Talk to Lizzy like she's awake," the nurse said while patting BJ on the shoulder and handing him a box of tissues.

"Lizzy, you mean the world to me. I never thought I would find a woman to love. I know I haven't told you that I love you yet, I was going to tell you tonight. Please wake up, so I can look you in those beautiful eyes and tell you how much I love you. I died inside when I saw that bull hit you. You are so very beautiful and smart and sexy—how could I *not* fall in love with you? I fell in love with you when you walked into the kitchen that first night I had dinner at the main house. If you remember, I couldn't talk. I love you Elizabeth Gordon, please wake up." The whole time BJ spoke to Lizzy he had been holding her left hand and stroking it. When he had finished talking he lifted her hand up and kissed it again.

His phone buzzed, he looked at the message, Sue and Jim had arrived at the hospital. He went out to look for them. Sue came up to him and gave him a cuddle, and she could see that he had been crying.

Jim gave him a hug and said, "Son, Lizzy will be alright, she is in the best place to be treated."

"Can we sit down please?" asked BJ. "You've both given me permission to marry Lizzy, but I haven't asked her yet. She means the world to me … I didn't think I would ever find a woman to love, let alone to marry. I haven't told Lizzy yet that I love her, and I'm worried she won't wake up so I *can* tell her."

"Son, stop. We know you love Lizzy, and you asked her to be careful before the muster. I heard her snap at you. I know from what she has asked Sue she has feelings for you, and I daresay she loves you as much as you love her. Why don't we go and see her?" Jim said.

They all went in to ICU to see Lizzy. BJ held her left hand again, and Sue gave her a kiss on the forehead and spoke softly to her. It was then BJ noticed Jim standing back.

"Jim, come over and stand here. I'll move to the end of the bed," BJ remarked.

Jim's looked so sad when he stood beside Lizzy. The doctor had been notified that Sue and Jim had arrived and he entered the room.

"Mr and Mrs Gordon, I take it. Could we talk out here please?" he asked and they walked out of Lizzy's room. He continued, "I suppose BJ has informed you of Lizzy's injuries. Our concern is she's not waking up. That could be because she knocked her head when she was thrown, but all her vital signs are good otherwise. I suggest you all stay with her for a little while then head to a motel and get some rest. If Lizzy wakes up or something happens we will ring you. We have all your phone numbers don't we?"

Sue gave the doctor their phone numbers so he could check them against Lizzy's records. She asked him for a recommendation for a motel they could contact at this late hour. He went to the desk and came back with the business card of a motel which was only three doors further down the street.

Jim phoned the motel and apologised about the late hour, fortunately he was able to rent two rooms. One for BJ and one for him and Sue.

Sue said she would prefer to stay with Lizzy, but the doctor said no. They went to the motel and Sue handed BJ a bag. He looked at the bag and then at Sue, "I went into your cabin and grabbed some clean clothes for you and your phone charger. Hope that was okay."

BJ was lost for words, so Jim filled the silence, "I was given your rifle before I left and locked it in my gun cupboard. This accident has upset all the guys, they were all talking on the radio as we left. One of them said if the bull hadn't already been dead a group would have gone out to find it. A few of the guys have buried Lizzy's horse and have made a cross out of sticks so Lizzy knows where her horse is laid to rest Jim paused for a moment, and then added, "Where did you learn to shoot like that, son? The pilot said the bull dropped in an instant, he saw it all from the chopper."

"I learnt to shoot down home. My nana was a dead-eye left-hander, she taught me well," BJ admitted.

"Well, let's get a coffee and hit the hay. I think tomorrow will be a big day," Jim remarked heading into the motel room.

CHAPTER FOURTEEN

BJ tossed and turned all night. He kept seeing the bull heading for Lizzy and then seeing her lying lifeless on the ground.

He got a few hours' sleep, woke early and headed for the shower. He'd not had a shower for a about a week because of being on the muster, and it felt so good! He washed away so much dust. BJ got out his fresh clothes and thankfully Sue had packed his spray deodorant. He heard a knock at the door, it was the breakfast tray arriving, and Sue was standing behind the lady delivering it.

"Bring your breakfast next door, BJ. No use you being on your own," she ordered, and BJ picked up his phone — now fully charged — his hat, his breakfast tray and room key.

"Morning, Jim, did you get any sleep?' he said.

"Nope, you?" Jim enquired. BJ let him know he only got a few hours.

"Sue, have you heard if Lizzy's engagement ring is ready for you to pick up?" BJ asked.

"Hold on," Sue got up and retrieved a small blue box from her handbag. She put the box on the table and BJ opened it.

"Christ, son, you have outdone yourself there!" Jim said.

"Hmm … and look at my old ring! Someone doesn't shop for jewellery for me," Sue said as a dig at Jim.

BJ was speechless, he couldn't believe how beautiful the ring was in real life.

"Thank you for all your help, Sue" he said. Sue had actually received Lizzy's engagement ring a few days earlier when an air courier delivered some goods from town. The ring was entrusted to the pilot who was to only hand it to Sue. They had just finished breakfast when Sue's phone rang.

"Hello, Mrs Gordon, just letting you know that Lizzy has woken up," it was a nurse from the hospital.

"Can we come up and see her now?" Sue enquired.

The nurse told her when visiting hours were, but given the situation it was fine for them to come up now. Sue told her they would be straight up.

Lizzy was sitting up in bed when they arrived and the doctor informed them she was going to be moved to a ward. Jim asked about a private room and was told there was one available.

BJ walked behind Jim and Sue and stayed outside the room until Lizzy was settled.

"Well, my girl, you have given us all a big shock. Do you remember anything at all?" Jim remarked.

"I remember the bull heading towards me and feeling him hit me, but after that I remember nothing," she said.

Jim called BJ into the room. He smiled at Lizzy, and he was so happy to see her smile back.

"Lizzy, BJ saw it all happen, he shot the bull just as it hit you. I'm sorry, Love, but your horse was killed when that bull barrelled into the both of you. BJ gave you first-aid and told everyone what to do. He didn't leave your side until last night when the doctor in ICU told us to go to the motel," Jim told her.

Lizzy looked sad; understandably, hearing that her horse had been killed upset her. "Lizzy, nothing could have been done to save your horse. It was dead before BJ got to you," Jim said while waving BJ to Lizzy's side.

"Okay, you young ones, we're going in search of a coffee. Would you like one, BJ?" Sue asked, and BJ nodded to her as Jim and Sue left the room.

BJ took Lizzy's hand, "Elizabeth Gordon, I nearly died when that bull hit you. And then when I found you unconscious I thought I had lost the chance to tell you how I feel about you. You really frightened me," BJ said while holding Lizzy's hand and stroking her fingers.

"BJ, thank you for everything, and I'm sorry I frightened you. I'm glad it was you who helped me … oh, you will have to sign my cast," Lizzy said with a grin.

"Done!" was all BJ said, as he signed the cast on her leg. The message was: *'Today, tomorrow, and forever I love you'.*

Lizzy read what BJ had written. A tear rolled down her cheek and he gently wiped it away, "Lizzy what's wrong?" he said in a worried voice.

"I didn't know you felt that way about me," Lizzy said.

BJ sat on the bed and held Lizzy's hand, "From the moment I met you I knew you were the one for me. Remember when we were sitting at the old house, I said, 'Like you, I think I have met the right person.' No, I damn well *know* I have. I haven't told you how I feel about you because we've been busy with work, then there was the whole thing with Kevin … oh, and our nights under the moonlight," BJ laughed.

Lizzy laughed too, and then admitted, "When Kevin tried that *shit* on me, I couldn't kiss him because I had feelings for you, but I didn't know how to tell you. That night—after how you sorted Kevin out—I knew then that I loved you so much. What's Mum and Dad going to say about us?"

"Well, we guessed a long time ago that there was something between you two." Lizzy and BJ had been so focused on each other, they had not noticed that Jim and Sue had returned with their coffees. "You should realise we're not blind," Sue said with a smile.

"You think your father goes to sleep when we're on the musters?! I've seen both of you sneak off, and I could hear the blokes talking about you. Gee, a couple of nights there you two got a bit hot!" Jim said with a grin and a laugh.

"What do you think of us though, is it okay with you?" Lizzy asked them.

"We're happy you've found someone you love," Sue remarked fondly.

"BJ, you just look after my girl, okay," Jim said.

Sue gave Jim a playful punch on the arm, "Really, Jim Gordon!"

"Jim, care for a walk outside? I need some fresh air," BJ said.

"Yep, I agree, not one for hospitals, give me the outdoors anytime."

"What's up, son?' Jim asked as soon as he and BJ left the building. "I feel like you have a question, or you need some advice."

"I'm so thankful to you and Sue for helping me with everything you've done. This accident has really frightened me. I hated seeing Lizzy hurt, and I felt powerless that I couldn't do anything to help her. I never had a father who I could talk to or ask for advice.

He's verbally abusive, and I find I can't talk to him about anything … never could. I don't know *how* to ask Lizzy to marry me, and I want to do it right. I don't want to lose her, Jim," revealed BJ.

"BJ, you did everything you could to help Lizzy, and if it wasn't for you jumping in and telling everyone what to do, well the situation may have turned out worse. If you ever need any advice or help all you have to do is ask me." Jim paused for a moment before continuing, "Now … the proposal. Gee, I just asked Sue one night, no special dinner, or flowers like they do now. With Lizzy, hmm … you have me thinking. I don't think she would want you to do anything huge. Can't take her riding for a while, but I might be wrong. Sue may have a better idea."

"I nearly asked her just now, but I didn't think it was the right place." BJ remarked. "I'm also wondering how I'm going to get back to the station, I don't have my ute here and, more importantly, how is Lizzy going to go sitting for hours in a ute? Surely, that isn't going to be the best for her."

"Will you slow down, son? One thing at a time. I was thinking the same thing. I think we should leave Sue here, and you and I drive back to the station together. I'll ask the doctor to get onto the Flying Doctor about getting Lizzy home, and if they can't do it I'm sure I can work something else out," Jim remarked. "Let's get back in there and see if they know how long Lizzy will be in here for." They both got up and walked back inside to Lizzy's room.

"Do you know where I can find the doctor please?" Jim asked the nurse.

"He will be into see Lizzy shortly," the nurse said.

Not long after Jim spoke to the nurse the doctor arrived. It was the same doctor who had treated Lizzy the previous evening.

"Hi, Lizzy, how are you feeling today?" the doctor asked.

"Okay, but I just want to go home, I hate hospitals and being in town. Please tell me when I can go home," Lizzy asked.

"I have looked at all your tests and your vitals are good. The broken leg will take time to heal, so you won't be able to do much for about eight weeks. Home … how far away is it again?" queried the doctor.

"We live on Emu Station, and it's about a three-hour drive from here," Jim told him.

"Normally I prefer to keep patients who have had a knock to the head in for a few days at least — just to make sure everything is alright. Your property is accessible by the Royal Flying Doctor Service, isn't it?" he asked.

"Dad built an airstrip and the Flying Doctor visits whenever they're needed. Why?" Lizzy asked.

"If the Flying Doctor can visit you occasionally to

check to make sure everything is progressing well, then I'm prepared to let you go home in a few days' time. However, there is *no* work for you for eight weeks. That includes no walking without crutches and definitely no horse riding. In eight weeks' time you will have to come back here for x-rays to confirm that everything has mended." Then the doctor turned to Sue, "Sue, I take it you will be looking after Lizzy?"

With a laugh and a smile Sue told the doctor, "Me, all the jackaroos, the cooks … everyone. If I need anything someone will be there. Will you organise the Flying Doctor to check on Lizzy? We're wondering how Lizzy is going to get back to the station. I don't think she can sit in a ute for three hours."

"The Flying Doctor can fly Lizzy back to the station. I am sure you have plenty of help to get her from the airstrip to home," the doctor said with a grin.

"Well, when can I go home?" Lizzy said, sick of all the talk, she wanted out. Out of the hospital.

"At least two more days in here, maybe three, then I will let you go home. I need to go and find out exactly when they can fly you home. I'll be back soon," the doctor said.

"What? Three more days! No, I want out now!" Lizzy said stubbornly.

The doctor left to call The Royal Flying Doctor Service to arrange Lizzy's flight home and her ongoing care. He returned a few minutes later. "Well, you are one lucky lady. I have organised everything and they can fly you out to your station in two days' time on an early morning flight," confirmed the doctor.

"Two days, no way! Today. I'm not staying here. You said all my vitals are good," Lizzy objected loudly. The doctor thought the daughter was just like the mother.

He went back to phone the Flying Doctor service again. At a pinch they could fly Lizzy home the following morning. He returned and told Lizzy what had been organised.

"Thank you," was all Lizzy said, before the doctor left the room. Jim followed him out and apologised for Lizzy's outburst.

"Boy, they are both strong ladies. Lizzy certainly got her point across," he said to Jim. They both laughed, and Jim thanked the doctor.

That night at the motel, BJ was having a coffee with Jim and Sue.

"Sue, why don't you stay with Lizzy, and BJ and I will drive home. Just let me know when you're leaving tomorrow so I will have some idea when to meet you at the airstrip. I'll get the blokes to bring another ute down and we'll put something in the back for Lizzy to lie on," Jim said. All three of them agreed to this plan.

Then BJ spoke to Sue, "I had a talk with Jim today about how and when to propose to Lizzy. He said you would have a better idea."

"Hmm … let me have a think about it," Sue answered thoughtfully.

"Okay, thanks Sue; and thank you both for everything you've done for me. I'm going to over to see Lizzy to let her know about the travel arrangements. It'll be hard not taking her home, but I know she will be in good hands," said BJ. "So, I'll see you nice and early, Jim, and I'll see you then too, *Mum,*" BJ said with a cheeky laugh.

CHAPTER FIFTEEN

Being 'farm' people, Jim, Sue, and BJ were always up early, and the following morning was no different. BJ and Jim left the motel about 5 am, but before they set off BJ said goodbye to Sue and told her he would see her when she and Lizzy arrived home.

BJ and Jim spoke about many different things on the way home, while Sue spent time with Lizzy. She noticed BJ's writing on Lizzy's leg cast.

"Well, do you love BJ?" she asked her.

"Yes I do, Mum. I've met the man I want to spend the rest of my life with," Lizzy replied.

Lizzy and Sue had a woman-to-woman talk about life, relationships, and marriage, and Lizzy brought up the subject of sex. Sue was quiet for a bit, and then said, "You know all about that, we had that talk long ago. Now, remember you aren't on the pill so before you start anything you better see the doctor for something." Nothing more was said about 'protection'.

BJ and Jim got home in time to fix things for Lizzy. They threw themselves into the work, changing the lounge room around, moving the coffee table so Lizzy had a table to rest her leg on. Then out to the ute to set up the tray for Lizzy to sit on comfortably from the airstrip back to the house.

"Time for a beer, BJ," Jim remarked, puffing.

Back at Stuart Hospital, the paramedics arrived with a patient trolley for Lizzy. Sue helped Lizzy dress in bike pants and a shirt, and she brushed her hair.

"Thanks, Mum, that feels so good. I'm glad you went and bought me some shorts and bike pants instead of a dress," Lizzy remarked.

"It's alright, I know you're not a fan of dresses. But you *will* have to wear a dress one day—if you know what I mean!" Sue said, smiling.

The paramedics helped Lizzy onto the trolley and secured the safety belts around her, just as the doctor arrived.

"Good morning to both of you, the Flying Doctor leaves in about an hour. I see the paramedics have taken care of you already. I'll finalise all your paper work for discharge shortly … I daresay you're excited to get home," the doctor said to Lizzy.

"I can't wait to get out of here. I think I'll be fine," she said with a grin, and continued, "I can't wait to see BJ,

I've missed him."

Sue had both bags—hers and Lizzy's—and stopped at the nurses' station to talk to the doctor.

"Mrs Gordon, here's all the paperwork regarding Lizzy. Included is what Lizzy can and can't do. Also, a list of phone numbers if you have any problems. Good luck to the both of you," he said, and the paramedic wheeled the patient trolley with Lizzy on it out of the ward and straight into a waiting ambulance. Sue sat in the front with the bags and chatted with the ambulance driver.

After a short drive they arrived at the airport and the ambulance backed up to the airplane. The nurse and doctor were the same ones who had flown with Lizzy to the hospital a few days previously. They greeted Sue and she showed them the paperwork from the hospital doctor.

"You wouldn't remember, because you were unconscious, but we're the crew who picked you up from the station the other night," the nurse said to Lizzy.

Lizzy thanked them both for everything they had done to help her, then Sue rang Jim to let him know they were about to leave.

Jim spotted the Flying Doctor airplane flying over the main house. He and BJ jumped into the ute and drove to the airstrip, while a couple of other blokes followed them in a second ute. The plane taxied up to the end of the runway, the doors were opened and the doctor and nurse stepped out. BJ said g'day to the doctor and the nurse, while Sue walked down the steps onto the airstrip. She walked over to Jim and gave him a kiss and a cuddle.

With the help of Jim, BJ, and the other two blokes, Lizzy was carefully transferred onto the tray of Jim's ute. Jim drove his ute and Sue sat in the front with him while BJ sat in the back holding Lizzy. The other two blokes returned to the main house in the other ute.

After a bit of a bumpy ride to the main house, Lizzy was glad to be home. She had been given crutches to use, but she also had to rest and elevate her leg as much as possible. BJ carried Lizzy inside to the lounge room.

"Lizzy, we're so glad you're home. We've set the lounge room up for you and there are pillows on the coffee table for you to put your leg up on," Jim said as BJ lowered her down on to the lounge.

"Beer, BJ?" Jim asked.

"I won't say no to one, thanks Jim," he replied.

After a beer Jim and BJ went back to work.

Lizzy hadn't enjoyed the hospital food and had hardly eaten any of it, so that night Sue cooked a roast dinner, as she knew that it was one of Lizzy's favourite meals—and, of course, BJ joined them.

He arrived at the main house freshly showered and dressed in clean clothes. Lizzy loved the smell of his deodorant—she always had.

After dinner BJ helped Sue clean up. Lizzy said she wanted to go out onto the verandah to see the night sky, so BJ helped her up and watched her closely as she used the crutches.

"Look at the stars, the sky is so clear … the air is so fresh …" Lizzy said.

"I love it here. It's different to home down south, but I feel really at home here now. No, this *is* my home now," BJ said. Lizzy was surprised to hear BJ say this, but she liked it.

After gazing at the night sky and talking for a while longer they headed inside, Lizzy said she was tired and was going to bed.

BJ helped her and when she got into bed, BJ gave her a kiss, "Sweet dreams, I love you so much," he said.

Lizzy replied, "I love you too."

BJ knew he had to ask *that* question soon, but when?

The other blokes who had been finishing up the mustering at *Bull's Head* arrived back a week later.

"Hi, Jim, all done, everything's taken care of. How is Lizzy going?" Harry asked.

"Thanks, Harry. Lizzy is getting there—just like me, she hates being sick. I'm going to see Cookie, and on the last Saturday night in October, I'm going to put on a big end-of-year barbecue. You'll need to get some Emu Station beef for the barbecue. I think we'll call it for the year once everything is done and put away," Jim said.

"Not a bad idea. Oh, you might want to talk to Old Jimmie, he's been a bit funny the last few days," Harry commented.

The next morning Jim went in search of Old Jimmie and found him looking at the sky.

"What's going on, Jimmie? Harry said you've been off for a few days," Jim remarked, looking at the sky himself.

"Rain coming … lots of it."

"You sure about that? There's not a cloud in the sky," Jim said, pointing to the sky.

"Yes, boss, the birds have been flying funny and the ants were moving. The clouds flying that way. Big lot of water coming," Jimmie said, definitely.

"How soon, Jimmie, before lots of water?" Jim asked.

"Couple of weeks, but rain before. See the cloud," Old Jimmie pointed to a small cloud.

"Yep, but it looks just like the others," Jim said.

"Me going home soon, river will be high," Old Jimmie

said while waving his hand up high.

"Okay, we might call it early. The last Saturday night this month, I'm putting on a barbecue, okay. Will you be there?" Jim asked.

"I will, but I go home after that. I see you next year in February, okay?" Old Jimmie said, and his bright white teeth shone as he smiled.

The end of the month was fast approaching. All the workers were now back from the camp and got stuck in and made sure all the machinery was serviced, and that all the fences around the homestead were secure. Nothing was left to chance, even down to some of the workers checking and fixing the floodways in case the wet season arrived early.

At breakfast time on the last Thursday in October, Jim walked into the cookhouse.

"Morning, everyone … and before you ask, Lizzy is going okay, just frustrated that she can't do anything. Now, my weather man here …" as he pointed to Old Jimmie, "… has said that we are going to get a lot of rain, so this Saturday night — yes, in three days' time — not tonight, I'm throwing an end-of-year barbecue, and after that most of you can head home. Your wages will be deposited into your bank accounts then." he said. There was plenty of cheering as most of them were glad to be going home.

Jim spoke to BJ, "BJ, Sue would like to see you at the house, don't know why." And immediately a chorus of 'You're in trouble!' echoed from the cookhouse.

BJ knocked on the glass door of the main house, "Morning, Sue, I hear you're looking for me?" he said.

"Yes, outside please!" she said, as she shooed BJ out. "With the end of the year coming I'm wondering if you're planning on heading home down south. Just want to know."

"Honestly, Sue, I haven't thought about it. With Lizzy down because of her leg, and with so much work on I just haven't had time to think about anything. Is there a reason why?" he asked.

"Because of Christmas and New Year, I just wanted to know that's all," she said. But BJ guessed there was something else she wasn't saying.

"Sue, spit it out, what's going on?" BJ asked in a firm but quiet voice.

"I know you're going to propose to Lizzy, and I know you'll want time alone together. So, I thought over the Christmas break one of the ladies and I would fix up the old governesses' quarters at the end of the main house. It's fully self-contained and it would be the perfect home for you and Lizzy," Sue said.

"Gee, I hadn't thought about that, but it would be nice just Lizzy and me," he said.

"What about this then? I'll fix up the place, and stock

it, and that can be our Christmas present to you and Lizzy. How's that sound?" Sue asked him.

"Thanks, Sue, that's really good of you! While I have you, I want to run something by you," BJ said while moving her away from the homestead.

BJ told Sue his idea of how he would propose to Lizzy.

"Don't worry, BJ, I'll get everything that's needed. I'll even bake the engagement cake and make up some excuse to Lizzy about it.

Meanwhile, Lizzy used the crutches with confidence now to move around the main house, and even to go outside. The sun felt so good on her skin, and she thought, *'I've been inside too long!'*

CHAPTER SIXTEEN

Sue arranged to get everything that was needed for the proposal. She even made a trip into Augustus Creek to buy it all, plus a little more. She helped Cookie put up Christmas decorations in the cookhouse and she explained why there were additional decorations and flowers, and a little of what BJ had planned. Cookie was excited and remarked, "Boy, this will make Christmas for everyone!"

On Saturday, BJ checked in with Sue to see how everything was going and to get her help with part of the proposal.

Because of the heat and humidity, he waited until just before he was to leave that afternoon to have a shower. He pulled on his best clothes and his hat and headed to the main house. Sue passed him the little blue box on the quiet.

Lizzy was dressed up—in a dress, no less—and this surprised BJ.

"Wow, don't you look beautiful!" BJ said admiringly

as he gave Lizzy a kiss.

"I hate dresses. I'll be glad to be back in jeans!" she replied.

"Soon, okay, it's a party," he told her.

Jim came into the kitchen, "Okay, everyone ready? Let's go before these blokes get out of hand," he said.

They all answered him, "Coming," but a few were a bit slower.

BJ hadn't seen the cookhouse or Cookie that day. Cookie had Christmas hats for everyone to wear and gave everyone a beer. Some of the blokes asked, "Do we have to wear this?"

"If you want this beer and you want to eat, then yes, you do have to wear it," he said while holding back the beer.

Because Sue had involved Cookie in the surprise, he had everything ready and he was in charge of the men. Harry and his wife and kids were there as well. It was all the employees together for once.

When Lizzy arrived she was asked many times, "Hi, Lizzy, how are you?" And her usual answer was "Okay, getting there, I want to get back to work though!"

Dinner had been eaten, or rather the tasty barbecue of Emu Station beef had been eaten and not a bit was left. Dessert had been served and everyone was talking and enjoying each other's company. Many were retelling all the funny stories from the year.

Because it was the station Christmas party and the en-of-year barbecue, Santa made an appearance. Little gifts were given out and the men were given new wallets or knives for work. Santa gave Harry's children gifts too. Sue had arranged for Santa to give Cookie a brand new knife set which had already been professionally sharpened.

"Holy hell! Thank you, Santa! Now, any of you blokes want a haircut?" Cookie joked.

"Well, to cap off the year we have something special. Lizzy, will you come and sit in Santa's chair please?" Cookie had done a great job getting one of the blokes to make Santa's chair. Santa announced that he had to leave and wished a Merry Christmas to everyone. Those who paid attention worked out that Santa was one of the labourers who coincidentally turned up back up at the barbecue after Santa left.

"Alright, Cookie, you know what to do," BJ said pointing at Cookie.

"Right, you loud mob, QUIET!! Come up here and take two flowers each: one for Sue and one for Lizzy. Thank you, Sue, for everything you have done this year, we all appreciate it so very much. Lizzy, we all love you and hope you recover real soon," Cookie said on behalf of all of them.

One by one, the blokes gave a flower and a peck on the cheek each to Sue and Lizzy. BJ was last, and as he gave Sue her flower, he whispered, "Thanks, Mum, for everything". He turned to Cookie who gave him a long box of roses for Lizzy.

"What the hell … what's going on?" was all Lizzy could say.

Phones came up, and cameras started recording and taking pictures …

BJ handed Lizzy the box of long-stemmed red roses, and she removed the lid and picked up the little blue box that was inside. She looked surprised and was lost for words. BJ gently took the little blue box from her and opened it to reveal a breathtaking engagement ring.

She looked at BJ and opened her mouth, but nothing came out. BJ was down on one knee and he held one of Lizzy's hands in his.

"Lizzy Gordon, you took my breath away the first moment I saw you. I love you so much. Will you marry me?" BJ said without stopping or losing his voice.

Lizzy had tears in her eyes and she opened her mouth, but still nothing came out. She swallowed, took a deep breath and said …

"Yes, yes, yes, I will marry you!" She finally got it out.

BJ leant forward and slid the ring onto Lizzy's finger, and it fitted her perfectly. They shared a kiss, and everyone was cheering and clapping. Many cameras flashed from all the photos being taken of Lizzy, BJ, and everyone else at the party.

Then Cookie came out with a crate of champagne and one of his workers brought out the engagement cake. "Right, because of Lizzy and her passenger, we have the cake on a wheelie table. Everyone come up and get some bubbly. Lizzy and BJ, it's time to cut the cake," ordered Cookie.

"Well that really caps the year off," announced Jim. "Does everyone have a drink? Here's to BJ and Lizzy!"

More photos were taken and questions were asked. Jim pulled BJ aside. "Okay, mate, tell me how the hell you pulled all that off. I didn't know a thing about it, other than for Lizzy to be in the Santa chair."

"Jim, I'm sorry I didn't tell you anything about it, but Sue helped me with everything and we wanted to keep it a surprise for everyone," BJ explained.

"Boy, that woman! … You look after my girl, son," Jim slapped BJ on the back and they went back to the party.

The night wore on and BJ asked Lizzy if she wanted to go back to the main house, and she said yes she would as she was tired. She held her dress while BJ lifted her out of the Santa chair. This brought whistles and clapping from the partygoers and Lizzy couldn't do anything but laugh at how BJ just picked her up like she weighed nothing.

"Watch it Jim, looks like they're eloping!" someone

yelled out and much laughter followed.

Jim and Sue just smiled, and Jim thanked everyone for their hard work, and said that he would see all of them next year.

Lizzy opened the sliding door into the kitchen and BJ walked through to the lounge and slowly sat Lizzy down. Before he could move Lizzy reached out and held his face.

"I love you, BJ, and I can't wait to marry you!" she said.

Their lips met and as they kissed Lizzy ran her hands over BJ; their kissing was urgent and when Lizzy's hands reached BJ's jeans button he stopped her.

"You don't realise how much I would love to take this further, but your mum and dad could walk in at any moment. Soon. The wait will be worth it," he said.

"I don't want to wait, but I know you're right," Lizzy said, taking a breath.

Not long afterwards Jim and Sue did walk in, carrying the leftover engagement cake.

"Well, what a surprise tonight turned out to be. BJ, I daresay you're glad you finally asked the question," Jim remarked.

"Yes, I am. Thanks to Sue for all her help, I couldn't have done it without her," BJ said.

"Yes, Mum, you didn't say a word to me, you left me

in the dark," Jim said, trying to sound like he was angry with Sue, and all she did was smile.

Jim and BJ grabbed a beer and headed out onto the verandah. Jim asked BJ about the heirloom ring he had down home that he'd spoken about before .

"I decided to get a new engagement ring for Lizzy, because I didn't have time to go back down south to get it," explained BJ. "My great, great grandma's ring needs fixing up before I give it to Lizzy. Who knows, it may be a wedding ring or an eternity ring, or even just an 'I love you' present."

Over the next few days, the workers left the station to go home. They said their goodbyes to Jim and Sue, and Lizzy and BJ.

Sue made a secretive start on BJ and Lizzy's *home,* making up excuses when Lizzy would question her about what she was doing.

The Flying Doctor had flown in a few times and checked on Lizzy over the previous weeks. At the final visit, in the first week of November, the Flying Doctor reminded Lizzy she needed to go to Stuart Hospital for x-rays to confirm that her leg was fully healed and to have the cast taken off.

BJ was worried about Lizzy sitting in the ute for nearly three hours for the drive to Stuart and raised this with the doctor. But the doctor said it would be fine as long as they had a few stops along the way.

BJ still hadn't thought much about going home for Christmas, he wanted to wait to see what the doctor said about Lizzy travelling. Now with the doctor's approval they made plans for him to drive Lizzy to Stuart Hospital the following week. It was going to be a two-day trip there and back, and Lizzy and BJ were looking forward to finally having some alone time. Time alone … totally by themselves. BJ felt his hormones already stirring at the thought of what could happen.

He decided to make a reservation for a nice motel room for them. When he phoned to make the booking he asked the receptionist if she could do something special for him and Lizzy, as they had just got engaged.

She said 'no worries', and made some suggestions to BJ; he agreed to her recommendations and happily paid for the extras. BJ could hardly wait. But first they had a long drive with Lizzy and her cast. He knew he would have to stop a few times along the way so an early start was important.

They left early in the cool of the morning, and BJ was thankful for the air conditioner Rick had installed in his ute the year before.

CHAPTER SEVENTEEN

The drive to Stuart turned out to be more manageable than Lizzy and BJ thought it would be. Following the doctor's orders, they stopped a few times along the way so Lizzy could get out and walk around for a while with the help of her crutches … and BJ, of course.

When they arrived in Stuart, BJ drove straight to the hospital for Lizzy's appointment at the outpatients' clinic. Her leg was x-rayed and it was confirmed that the fractures had healed fully, so her cast was removed. Lizzy felt relieved to have the plaster cast off and was pleased that everything had healed well. She was given strict instructions about what she could and couldn't do for the next few weeks.

With the hospital appointment out of the way, BJ drove to the motel where he had booked a room for them. He was hoping that the extra special things he had requested for Lizzy were in place.

They checked-in and decided to have lunch in the motel restaurant before going to their room. After the early start and the hospital appointment they were both hungry.

When Lizzy opened the door of their motel room she noticed rose petals scattered on the floor. A big bunch of red roses was in a vase on the table, and when she went into the bathroom the bath tub had a basket of roses petals beside it.

"This is too much!" she said as she walked out of the bathroom. When she spotted BJ with a rose in his mouth, she laughed, and he laughed too. The long wait was finally over.

BJ took Lizzy in his arms and kissed her with an intensity he couldn't deny any longer … Lizzy responded with the same urgency and pulled BJ's shirt open, then she let her hands slide all over his back and chest. She kissed his body all over and when she got to his nipples she gave each one a light flick of her tongue. She continued to kiss him while she undid his jeans and slid his underpants down towards the floor setting his erect penis free. BJ had kicked off his boots when they came into the room, so his jeans fell to the floor. Lizzy's hands cupped him, and she gently played with his already hardened erection. BJ's breath was taken away momentarily, he enjoyed the feelings going through his body.

BJ lifted Lizzy up to kiss her on her lips and her neck, while lifting her shirt up over her head and taking it off her. Lizzy's firm breasts needed no bra, and BJ saw the beauty of them for the first time. He then lifted Lizzy up and gently laid her down on the bed. He continued to kiss her all over and when he got to her breasts he gave each one a tantalising kiss until he reached her nipples. His tongue gave each erect nipple a soft, gentle lick of his tongue finishing with a gentle kiss where her nipple was in his mouth.

He continued down her body and when he reached her shorts he slid them and her lacy underpants off. He kissed and fondled her now-moistened mound, and then his tongue found her pleasure bud. Lizzy moaned, this was something she had never experienced before. The sensations that rocked her body were new to her and she loved it all: their passionate, sensual-sexual kissing, the discovery of each other's bodies, and how they felt in the heat of the moment. They experienced the feel of each other's bodies being so close, until neither of them could hold on any longer. Lizzy shifted her body to allow BJ's erection to slide into her.

They had waited a long time to surrender to their desire and now their bodies were intertwined, sweaty from the intensity of it. They took their time, neither of them was in any hurry for it to end, all the while building to the point when they were both overcome with overpowering orgasms.

BJ held Lizzy in his arms and they lay together in the warmth of their love, not wanting to break the magic of what had just happened. Eventually, they climbed into the shower to cool off, but they couldn't hold back the tide of their lust and began making long, passionate love all over again.

Afterwards they lay naked on the bed together, and were thankful for the cool breeze from the air conditioning washing over their bodies. They soon fell asleep from exhaustion and contentment until BJ was woken by the sound of Lizzy's phone ringing.

"Shit, it's your mum! Quick, get dressed," BJ said urgently.

BJ answered the phone "Hi, Mum, Lizzy is in the loo … hang on she'll be here in a sec."

"How did she go at the hospital?" Sue asked.

"No cast, but no work or riding for a while … oh here she is," BJ said as he handed the phone to Lizzy.

"Oh my God … men! BJ, this is a video call, don't you know how to do that? Sorry, Mum. Men!" Lizzy adjusted the phone and continued, "There we go, now I can see you. Yes, I no longer have the rigid cast on, but I'll have a soft foam cast for a little while. Still no work or riding or walking on it at the moment. The Flying Doctor has to check on me for another couple of months, that's as long as it doesn't rain and they can still land on the airstrip, of course."

"I bet you're both enjoying the time away from the station, you know we have to celebrate your engagement properly. When you get home we'll have to talk about a party,"

"Really, Mum?!" Lizzy said.

"Yes, but we'll talk when you get home. Can I speak to BJ for a second? Love you, Lizzy." Lizzy passed to phone to a now-dressed BJ.

"Hi, Mum, what's up?" BJ asked.

"Could you pick up a few things for me please while you're there? I'll send you a text message with the details of where to go, they'll have the order ready for you when you get there," Sue said.

"No worries, we'll see you tomorrow," BJ said as they ended the call.

"Boy that was close," BJ said.

It was now nearly dinner time, so they got ready to go down to the restaurant, BJ was looking forward to having a romantic dinner with Lizzy. The restaurant was lovely at night with romantic candlelit lighting, so they chose a quiet table in the far corner.

Halfway through dinner BJ felt a foot slide up his leg.

"Hmm … someone is horny again then?" BJ whispered as he leaned forward.

"Yep, can't wait to get you back to the room," Lizzy said playfully.

"You do know when we go home we won't be able to make love. I don't know if your dad would be okay with us being together under his roof or any roof.

"Leave them to me, I know Mum would be okay with it. Maybe we could move into the little house out the back of the cabins," Lizzy said.

Little did she know Sue had nearly finished setting up the flat, where the governess use to live, just for them.

BJ had a lot to think about. Did he take Lizzy home for Christmas, or did he stay up north for Christmas?

"I have a question," started BJ. "When I started this job I was always going to go home for Christmas. Now with Paul passing I would really like to go home to see Beth and Bree and Cody, and my other mates too. What do you think of a trip away? Only thing is, if it rains we won't get back to Emu Station until … oh … February."

"Hmm … I hadn't thought of you going home. I would love to meet Bree. Mum knows how to read all the weather charts so why don't we look at everything when we get home? Let's talk to Mum and Dad about it then. How's that sound?" Lizzy asked.

After the meal they returned to their room and unsurprisingly another night of long, passionate, and heated sex. They managed a few hours of sleep, and in the morning BJ woke Lizzy by kissing her body and caressing her breasts. Lizzy stirred and moaned with pleasure. They kissed and caressed one another knowing without question that it would lead to them making love … again.

When they were finished BJ smiled at Lizzy and

remarked, "Morning, Mrs O'Brien-to-be!" Lizzy kissed him good morning and headed for the shower. After breakfast they left to go back to the station, but on the way BJ had to pick up the shopping Sue ordered.

"What has Mum ordered there?" Lizzy asked.

"Don't know, but you know your Mum …" BJ said. thinking to himself, *If you only knew.*

CHAPTER EIGHTEEN

After about three hours of driving, and with the heat of the day now in full force, BJ and Lizzy were glad to arrive back at the station.

"Hi, you two," Sue said, welcoming them back.

Jim came out from the main house and said hello to them too, and then he and BJ unloaded the ute.

Inside the house was nice and cool; Sue had already made lunch, and an ice-cold jug of soft drink awaited them.

"It's good you don't have your cast on anymore. Did you save it?" Sue asked knowing full well what BJ had written on it.

"Yes, I did, Mum. And it feels great to have it off. I have to put moisturiser on my leg regularly and still not do too much on it for the time being though," Lizzy told her.

Jim and BJ returned quietly from putting Sue's order into the little flat she was fixing up for BJ and Lizzy.

"She is getting hot out there already!" Jim commented.

He noticed a grin between Lizzy and BJ, "What are you two thinking? Are you holding back on something?" Jim asked curiously.

"Well, it's about Christmas and New Year," BJ explained. "Lizzy and I were talking, and I always thought I would go home for Christmas, but I know what Old Jimmie said to you about the big rain, Jim. Sue, Lizzy said you had access to online weather charts. We were wondering if it would be alright with both of you if Lizzy and I headed to Chilly, leaving in about a week's time?"

Jim turned to Sue, "Mum, what do you think? Do you think the wet will hold off until then? Have you heard if Peter is coming home?"

"No, Peter's not coming home. I think it will be alright, but what about your leg, Lizzy?" Sue asked.

"We have a good doctor and a small hospital in Chilly, so they can look after anything Lizzy needs," suggested BJ. "I only have to ring Mum to make sure there's room for us. Anyway, if there isn't I know Johnno and Jenny at the pub, or the motel will have a room for a while. I can easily call them."

"It's okay with us," Jim and Sue both said.

Sue logged on to her computer and checked all the relevant weather data and predictions. It didn't look like the monsoon had formed yet, or that a cyclone was threatening. So BJ and Lizzy made arrangements to leave Emu Station in about a week's time and kept a watch on the weather in the meantime. If they were flooded out they couldn't return until possibly late January or early February the following year.

The next morning BJ rang his mum.

"Hi, Mum, how are you going?"

"Fine, son. How are you doing up there? We were only talking about you last night, wondering if you are coming home for Christmas," she said.

"I'm good, Mum. I am coming home for Christmas and New Year. Just wondering if my room will be free or is everyone coming home?" BJ asked.

"Everyone is coming home, and your brother has already moved into your room so, unfortunately, your room is taken. We can always put a tent up in the back yard for you or you can sleep in your tent on your ute," BJ's mum suggested.

"Well, I'm bringing home a friend so the tent will be no good. I'll ring the motel. See you all soon," BJ said.

BJ rang the motel, and luckily he got the last room available. It was actually the business suite, which was a bigger room than the normal motel room. He paid a deposit, and asked them not to let any of the locals know about his booking.

Then BJ rang his friend, Rick, "Hi, mate, how are you going down there?" he asked.

"Great to hear from you, mate, I'm going good, busy. The town has more people in it since you left. Some of the farms have been sold and had houses built on them. So I'm even busier than before. How have you been up there?" Rick asked in an excited voice, he was so happy to hear from BJ.

"I'm going well. Now, you're not to tell anyone that I'm coming home for Christmas and New Year, and I won't be by myself. No one knows but you, I'm engaged to a beautiful lady and she's coming with me," BJ said.

"Mate, congratulations! It will be great to meet your lady. What's her name?" Rick asked, all excited, before adding, "When are you looking at getting here?"

"Her name's Lizzy. We're looking at leaving soon, hope to be home in about a week or so," BJ said.

They ended the call and BJ went over to the main house to talk to Lizzy.

"Hi, gorgeous. How are you going getting your stuff together for us to head south?" BJ asked.

"I nearly have everything together. I'm so looking forward to meeting everyone … plus we'll be alone again," she whispered excitedly.

BJ went into the kitchen to find Sue, "Sue, is Jim around?" he asked.

"Jim, where are you?" Sue called out, and Jim came into the kitchen from the office.

"Yes, what do you want, Mum?" he said.

BJ spoke up, "Morning, Jim, I want to talk to you again about Lizzy and me heading south for Christmas and New Year. I understand if it rains we won't get back in for a while. I just wanted to double-check you are okay with that."

"If you want to go home that's fine, as long as Lizzy is okay to travel that far, considering her recovery from her leg fracture," Jim said. "I understand if the monsoon breaks you won't get back here, but we'll deal with that later. You still thinking of leaving in a week's time?"

"Yep, that's our plan," confirmed BJ." Do you have any work for me to do until then?"

"Work wise you have nothing, unless Sue needs anything. You can use whatever you need to get your ute ready to go."

"Thanks Jim, and don't worry, I'll look after Lizzy," BJ said.

Lizzy and BJ sat down with a map and worked out where they could stop each night. When they had made a decision about motels Lizzy booked the rooms online for them.

They decided to make it a four-day trip home, allowing extra time for stops for Lizzy to stretch her legs. BJ gave Lizzy a kiss and said he would see her later, then he went and checked over his ute, and gave it a clean. He thought he would look at upgrading to a new 4x4 soon, even though he still loved his ute.

Because the cook had gone home, BJ was having his meals at the main house. One morning after breakfast, Sue and Jim said they had a surprise for Lizzy and BJ. Sue winked at BJ, meaning she had finished their little home.

"Because you're both heading to Chilly for Christmas, Sue and I have your Christmas present ready for you early. Can you follow us please?" Jim announced.

"What's going on?" Lizzy asked, walking with the aid of the crutches down the long verandah of the house.

"This is from Dad and me. Merry Christmas to the both of you!" Sue said opening the door of the little flat.

"Wow, holy hell!" Lizzy said, amazed. She looked in through the doors and saw that Sue had furnished the flat with everything they would need to be comfortable. Sue had turned the air conditioning on earlier so it was lovely and cool. There was a lounge and a coffee table, and to the side near the kitchen there was a round table and chairs. The table had a vase with a small bunch of wildflowers in it that Sue had picked from the property, and it all looked so homely. Lizzy was so surprised at what Sue had done, everything was decorated just how she would have done it herself.

"The governesses' flat was sitting empty, and now

you're engaged we decided you need a home of your own."

Jim added, "Here are the keys to your new home. You can move your things in before you head south, and when you come back it will be ready for you to move straight into. Looks like you'll have plenty of work on today, BJ, moving your things and Lizzy's things in here."

"Jim and Sue, thank you so much!" BJ said.

"No, from now on its Mum and Dad, okay?" announced Sue.

Lizzy gave her mum and dad a big cuddle to say thank you. That day, with Jim's help, Lizzy and BJ packed up all their belongings and moved them into their new home.

After dinner that night, even though they both were tired … they were looking forward to time alone.

CHAPTER NINETEEN

It was now late November and BJ and Lizzy were looking forward to the trip to Chilly. Time alone, catching up with everyone, and for BJ to be able to introduce Lizzy as his fiancée.

BJ loaded the ute with his and Lizzy's belongings, then early the next morning they left Emu Station for the long drive to Chilly. They stopped a few times each day for Lizzy to stretch her legs and sometimes for fuel too.

After four days on the road, BJ drove into Braham. He decided that they would spend the night there and in the morning leave for The Flats, Bree's farm where she and Cody lived, in Chilly. Chilly used to be home for BJ, but now Emu Station was home.

BJ showed Lizzy part of the town of Braham; not much to show, but it was different to Augustus Creek. They had lunch and Lizzy lay down to rest her leg for a bit back at the motel. They were both tired after their long days on the road and before too long they fell asleep.

The next morning they left Braham heading towards The Flats. When they were just before Dutchman's Road, BJ pulled over and stopped the ute.

"See the big gum tree over there … that's where Bree had her accident. It was just after that when Cody told Bree he loved her. Just like us," he said.

"Boy, that's a big gum tree. Bree's lucky she wasn't seriously injured," Lizzy remarked, looking at the size of the tree.

After about an hour, BJ pulled into The Flats. He blasted the horn a couple of times when he saw Cody, Bree, and Beth standing at the backyard gate.

"Hi, everyone!" BJ said while walking around the ute to open the door for Lizzy. When they saw Lizzy their mouths fell open.

"Welcome home, BJ!" a chorus of voices said.

"Hi, I'm Beth. Let me help you sweetheart—inside everyone!" Beth instructed, helping Lizzy on one side while BJ helped her on the other side.

"Well, BJ, who is this lovely lady?" Cody asked, not letting on he that he already knew who Lizzy was.

"Everyone this is Lizzy … my fiancée," BJ said, while holding Lizzy's hand. Cody and Bree and Beth were in shock. Cody had known about Lizzy, but not about the engagement. They all came forward with a cuddle and congratulated BJ and Lizzy.

"Come on, coffee everyone?" Beth asked, and with

that it was coffee all round.

"Bree, BJ has spoken a lot about you, how you deal with running the farm, and also about how you deal with what happened to you," Lizzy said.

Bree said laughing, "I hope it was all good!" and then she asked to see Lizzy's engagement ring.

"Well, BJ, you've kept this a secret. The last I knew was that Lizzy was in hospital after the bull charged her," Cody said.

"It's just like what happened with you and Bree, the accident woke me up to what was in front of me," BJ said.

"BJ, son, how long have you both been engaged?" Beth asked.

BJ and Lizzy told them all about how they met and fell in love and then got engaged after the accident. Lizzy was laughing about BJ asking her dad for her hand in marriage.

"Well, that is respect for you. Your Nana Grace brought you up right, BJ!" Beth said.

"Mum, I'm really sorry I didn't get home for Paul's funeral, we were out on a big muster," BJ explained gently to Beth while holding her hand.

"BJ, what was it you told Dad and me that Paul said to you the last time you saw him?" Lizzy asked.

BJ gave a laugh, picked up his coffee and held it up to

the kitchen ceiling, "Yes, Paul, I did bring home a wife from up there. Oh, nearly a wife," he remarked, and everyone laughed heartily.

Beth got up and went into the lounge room and came back with some items. Handing them to BJ she said in a quiet voice, "Paul left these for you in his will."

Paul had left BJ his whip, his old rifle, his pocket knife, his hat, and a letter.

BJ was quiet, he looked at the items and his eyes filled with tears. Beth reached out and held his hand. "Come on, son, no tears. Paul would not want that, he would be going off about that in his usual way," Beth said, with care.

"Come on, Lizzy, let's go and sit on the verandah," suggested Bree. "Here, I'll get your coffee for you." The two women went out onto the verandah to talk in private, away from the blokes.

"BJ has spoken a lot about you Bree, and I can tell that you're special to him," Lizzy said.

Bree opened up to Lizzy about her friendship with BJ and told her about all the things they done together over the years. She assured Lizzy there was only friendship between them, but even so, she cared deeply for BJ. With the air cleared between them, the subject changed to other things. About an hour later Beth came out onto the verandah and announced it was lunchtime.

"Let me help you, Beth," Lizzy said.

"No, you are a guest, and in my home you don't do anything," she said, and Lizzy thanked her.

They enjoyed a lovely homecooked lunch together, and afterwards BJ and Lizzy were heading out to Rick's auto shop. As they were leaving to go, Bree reached out to Lizzy and said quietly, "Here's my phone number, if you need anything or just want a girls' day out, call me." The two women hugged each other warmly, and Lizzy whispered her thanks to Bree.

It was a short drive from The Flats to Rick's auto shop in Chilly.

"Hey, you're home, BJ! Who is this lovely lady?" Rick asked, grinning.

"Rick, this is Lizzy, my fiancée," BJ explained while Rick was embracing Lizzy.

"What? Oh my God, what a surprise! Congratulations to both of you," Rick exclaimed, proud of himself that he hadn't given away that he already knew about the engagement.

They had so much to catch up on and they talked for a while, then Rick asked, "What are you two doing for dinner tonight?"

"We're booked into the motel, and Lizzy needs to rest this leg up, so we'll grab something and eat in the motel room," BJ said.

"Hey, why don't I get Jenny from the pub to deliver you dinner? Anything you like, the menu hasn't changed, mate. My treat, just tell me the number of your room. Jenny will be so pleased to see you," Rick said.

BJ and Lizzy checked out the pub menu on their phones and gave Rick their order. Rick gave them both a hug and BJ promised Rick he would catch up with him again soon.

Dinnertime came around and there was a knock on the door. BJ opened it to see Jenny standing there with their meals, smiling. He introduced Jenny and Lizzy to one another and then gave Jenny a hug while thanking her for the food. As Jenny was leaving he promised that they would catch up with her the following night at the pub.

After dinner, BJ got out Paul's letter and read it.

Dear BJ,

If you're reading this letter it means I have passed on.

I know I never told you, but you have been like a son to me. You're a quiet man, but you're loyal and caring and nothing was ever too much for you to do for me or anyone else.

All the campfires we shared, the barbecues, and all the times you've been out here at The Flats were special.

Son, I've left you my whip, my old rifle, my pocket knife and my hat. I know you'll get a lot of use out of them in your new job.

When you said you were going up north to work, it felt like I was losing a son, but I understood why you had to go. I hope you make a good life for yourself up there, and don't worry about what anyone says, it's your life.

Have a beer for me and remember—no drink driving! Enjoy your life and stay safe.

Paul

P.S. Oh, and make sure you bring a wife home from up there!

After reading the letter BJ was unusually quiet, and he hung his head. BJ was really going to miss Paul; he had been a special person in his life.

"You okay?" Lizzy asked.

"Yes, thanks, I'm fine," and with that BJ put the letter away.

It had been a long day and both of them were tired so they went to bed early.

Over the next few weeks BJ visited family and friends and introduced Lizzy to all of them. They spent a day going through his belongings at his mum's and dad's house. He was deciding what to take back up north because Emu Station was home from now on. Home with Lizzy. BJ's mum gave him his great, great grandmother's ring and he showed it to Lizzy.

"It's beautiful!" she said, as she looked admiringly at the ring. When Lizzy gave the ring back to him, BJ placed the ring back into its box and put it in the briefcase where he kept all his important documents and paperwork. Even though he had already given Lizzy a beautiful engagement ring he would have this one remodelled just for her. He would talk to Sue about it when he got back up to Emu Station.

CHAPTER TWENTY

It was now Christmas week, and Lizzy hadn't been feeling well for a few days. She wondered if all the travelling so soon after her accident had taken its toll on her. She didn't say anything to BJ, but she knew something wasn't right, so she phoned Bree just after breakfast.

"Hi Bree, I'm just wondering if you're free today. I'd like to see a doctor and I believe the clinic at the hospital here is a good one."

"Are you okay, Lizzy?" Bree asked.

"Don't know, it may be nothing. I don't want to worry BJ unnecessarily."

"I'll come over this morning and take you to the hospital, see you about 9 am." Bree said.

Lizzy told BJ that she and Bree were going out for coffee, and that she wanted to check out the gear at the produce store too.

Bree arrived promptly at 9 am and drove Lizzy to the hospital. Lizzy still had all the paperwork with her from her stay in hospital up at Stuart.

They checked in with a nurse when they arrived, and after a short wait a doctor came out to the waiting room.

"Hi Bree, how are you today?" he asked, smiling. "Now, I take it you are Lizzy Gordon? In the room please," the doctor directed Lizzy towards the consulting room.

"Bree, would you come in with me please?" Lizzy asked.

"You sure?" Lizzy nodded.

The consultation was thorough, the doctor spoke with Lizzy at length, did a physical examination and then left the room while he ran some tests. When he returned he was smiling.

"Lizzy, I have some news for you. You're about six weeks pregnant, and your baby is due around the 17th of August."

Both Lizzy and Bree were shocked. The doctor asked Lizzy a few more questions and it was decided he would do an ultrasound to make sure everything was on track.

"Yep, see that little peanut? Well, that's your baby. Is the dad on the scene at the moment? I know you're visiting from up north," he asked Lizzy.

Bree spoke up, "The dad is BJ, doctor."

"Do you mean BJ O'Brien?" he asked.

"Yes, that's my fiancé, and this will be a good Christmas present for him. Can I get a picture of 'Peanut' please, doctor?" Lizzy asked. Now that the shock of an unexpected pregnancy had worn off she was delighted about it.

After the doctor's appointment, Bree and Lizzy went to have a coffee at the produce store.

"Bree, can you keep this quiet for now? I noticed BJ needs a new wallet and I love the leather ones in the glass case over there. I thought of buying one of them and putting the picture of Peanut in it." Lizzy said.

"No worries, I'll keep it a secret. Congrats as well." Bree took a sip of her coffee and then said, "Hold on, stay here, I'll get the wallets and bring them over so you can choose which one you want for BJ."

Lizzy chose a leather wallet with an engraved design on it. After they finished their coffee they went back inside the store and Lizzy looked at a few other items as well. She picked up a shiny silver belt buckle and showed it to Bree, "I love this!" she exclaimed before putting it back down. "Maybe next time … I have other priorities now."

Lizzy was enjoying spending some time browsing through all the merchandise at the produce store. "Bree, where are the halters? When I got hit by the bull the guys took all the gear off my horse, but I don't think the halter survived the impact," Lizzy said.

"Over here, Lizzy, I love this halter. What bit do you use?" Bree asked her.

"I love that halter too, and it has a snaffle bit, just like the one I use. I'll take the halter and this wallet please. How much do I owe you?" Lizzy asked.

"You can have a staff discount on me," and Bree calculated the cost of the two items. After Lizzy paid for the halter and wallet, Bree drove Lizzy back to the motel.

"You can tell Cody about Peanut, but he's to say nothing to anyone. I'm going to give BJ the wallet with Peanut's ultrasound image in it on Christmas Day. Thanks for everything today, Bree, and please don't forget to keep my secret safe," Lizzy said.

Christmas Day arrived a few days later. "Merry Christmas, sweetheart," BJ said to Lizzy as he gave her a small box.

She opened it to find the belt buckle she had loved in the produce store. Along with it was a gold bracelet that had a heart with a diamond inset into it.

"They are beautiful, BJ! Thank you so much … I love them." Lizzy said.

She handed BJ his present, he opened it up and saw the wallet, "I love it, it's just what I need, thank you."

Lizzy smiled and said, "Look inside!"

BJ took the wallet out of its box and opened it up. He pulled out the ultrasound image and he stared at it for a moment.

"Are you … does this mean … are you?" BJ tried to talk, but the words just wouldn't come out properly.

"Yes, we're having a baby! We're going to be parents," Lizzy said with a broad smile.

"Are you sure?" was all BJ could say, so Lizzy told him the truth about the 'day out' with Bree and she pointed to the ultrasound image and said that's 'Peanut'.

BJ hugged Lizzy, he had never been happier in his life.

"I couldn't ask for a better Christmas present. Oh, what will your mum and dad say?" BJ asked. Lizzy laughed and reassured him that they would be fine about it.

Bree sent a text message to her mum and dad to turn on the computer so they could have a video call.

"Merry Christmas, Mum and Dad! How is it up there?" Lizzy asked.

"Dry, no rain yet," Jim said.

"BJ, you're quiet!" Sue said.

"Well … we have a special Christmas present for you both," and with that Lizzy held up the picture of Peanut.

"What the hell is that?!" Jim remarked.

Sue's eyes filled with tears and one trickled down her

cheek. Jim saw this and wondered what was wrong.

"Jim, you silly old bugger! Does that mean we are going to be grandparents?" Sue asked with a shaky voice.

"Yes, Nana and Pop. BJ and I are expecting. I only found out earlier this week. The baby is due around the middle of August, so when we get back we'll have to organise a nursery in our new home." Lizzy said smiling.

Sue and Jim were genuinely happy. They all talked for a little while longer and agreed that Lizzy and BJ would let them know when they were leaving Chilly to head back home, before they ended the video call.

BJ was quiet, then suddenly he looked up to the ceiling.

"Are you okay, BJ?" Lizzy asked reaching out for his hand.

"Yep, I'm thinking how lucky I am. First your dad took a chance on me to work up north when I had no experience working up there. Then I met you and fell in love with you, and now I'm going to be a dad. Earlier this year I would never have dreamed of any of it. I love you, Lizzy Gordon … and I love you too, Peanut!"

CHAPTER TWENTY-ONE

"You there, Mum?" BJ called out to his mum as he and Lizzy walked through the front door of his parents' home.

"Hi BJ, hi Lizzy, Merry Christmas," his parents chorused. As usual there were hugs all round, and questions asking what they all had received for Christmas.

"Lizzy gave me a great Christmas present," BJ announced, and with that he showed his mum and dad the ultrasound image of Peanut.

"What the hell is that?" his dad said loudly and roughly.

"We're expecting!" explained BJ.

It was not the usual congratulations they had expected, and then the questions came thick and fast. BJ was upset and hurt that what had been a happy event for everyone ended with his dad running him down. As usual.

BJ had been at the receiving end of his dad's verbal abuse for many years, and this was the last straw.

"Dad, enough. I've taken your abuse for too many years, and you are not going to behave in that manner in front of Lizzy and my baby. I'm sick and tired of the way you talk to me. I am done!"

BJ then turned to Lizzy and said, "Come on, Lizzy, let's go out to the shed."

When they reached the shed Lizzy took BJ's hand and asked, "Are you alright, BJ? Thank you for standing up for me and Peanut, but what are we doing here?"

"I'm going to get everything I own and I'm never coming back. I am done. Enough!" And with that BJ loaded all his belongings onto his ute.

BJ's mum found them at the shed, "BJ, what are you doing?" his mum asked.

"Enough! I'm done. From now on my home is Emu Station. I won't take that shit from Dad anymore and I won't have him upset Lizzy. So, this is goodbye, Mum." BJ's mum pleaded with him to ignore his dad, but BJ stood firm and repeated that he was done.

BJ and Lizzy drove away from his parents' home and made their way to the The Flats, Bree's and Cody's property. As they were driving along Lizzy asked BJ if he was alright.

"I will be fine. Emu Station is home for me now, and after what just happened I can't wait to get home, home with you and Peanut and Mum and Dad."

Lizzy grabbed BJ's free hand and kissed it. "You know

that I'm here, and I always will be." she said.

"Merry Christmas, everyone!" BJ said, walking in the back door at The Flats. There were warm hugs all around and then Beth offered everyone coffee. She could see BJ was upset and took him aside and asked him quietly why. He told her that his father had been verbally abusive, yet again, and that he wasn't going to take it anymore.

Beth remarked, "BJ, be happy and don't think about your father. You have Lizzy now. One day he will wake up to himself." Beth gave him a big hug and added, "Let's enjoy the day while we can, because I'm going to miss you both when you go back to the station."

"I got the best Christmas present out," and with that BJ pulled out the scan of Peanut, and Beth asked, "What is that?"

"Mum, that is my Christmas present: 'Peanut'. Lizzy and I are going to be parents." Bree winked at Lizzy.

Shock, excitement, hugs. Beth had tears in her eyes and was tightly hugging BJ and Lizzy.

"What do you think Paul would say, Mum?" BJ whispered.

"He would be happy. Well, you brought home a wife *and* a baby," Beth said.

Lizzy pulled Bree aside, "Thank you for everything,

Bree. And look at what BJ gave me for Christmas — it's the silver belt buckle I loved and nearly bought."

"Okay you two, what are you doing for Christmas lunch?" Beth asked Lizzy.

"Honestly I don't know, I know it won't be at BJ's parents' place." she replied. Lizzy filled Bree in on what happened with BJ's dad, and how she was worried about BJ.

"Lizzy, BJ's dad has always been rude to him, and I've seen him in tears over what his father has said before. I'm proud he has taken a stand … and you and BJ are staying *here* for lunch!" Bree decided.

Lizzy hugged Beth and offered to help her, but was told, no, everything was nearly ready. So, with a bit of time before lunch would be ready, the four of them — BJ and Lizzy, and Cody and Bree — checked out the farm for a bit.

"Cody, can I ask you something?" BJ asked quietly. "Do you and Bree have any room in the shed where I can store my stuff? After what Dad said, I grabbed all my gear and left — I'm never going back there."

"Come on, mate, drive me up to the shed and we'll unload whatever you're not taking back up north. We'll look after it all for you," Cody replied, placing a hand on BJ's shoulder.

Christmas lunch was delicious, and questions were asked about the station and everything about the north. There was laughter about what had happened the previous year with the low-lifes at The Flats, and with Kevin at Emu Station.

"So, *when* are you going to get married and *where* are you going to get married?" Bree asked.

"We haven't even discussed that," Lizzy said.

"Well after Dad's drama today … hmm …" BJ said, while looking at Lizzy, "I would like to get married on the station."

Lizzy gave BJ a hug and said, "Yes! I would love that!"

"So that means you guys will have to come up north," BJ added, "we haven't set a date, but we have Peanut on the way."

Lizzy and Bree moved out onto the verandah, and Lizzy started the conversation, "I would love to chat online with you when I get home, Bree. From what BJ has told me you don't have a lot of girlfriends, and I don't have any, just the station. Would you be okay with that?"

"Lizzy, that would be great! I guess you won't be riding or mustering next year, and it would be great to hear how you are both going." Bree gave Lizzy a hug, it was a nice change to have a genuine girl-friend.

Later that afternoon BJ and Lizzy returned to the motel. "Are you missing home, Lizzy?" BJ asked.

"Yes, I am, but these are your friends and this was home for you," responded Lizzy.

"This is not home for me anymore, even though I have good friends here. How do you feel about heading home to the station?"

Lizzy gave BJ a hug and said, "Let's go!"

The next morning BJ and Lizzy gave Sue and Jim a video call.

"Hi Mum and Dad, how are you both?" Lizzy asked.

"We're fine. How are both of you?" Sue said. Lizzy told them what happened at BJ's parents' house and Jim shook his head in disgust.

"You okay, BJ?" Jim asked.

"I will be fine, Jim … what's the rain situation up there?"

"We haven't had any rain. They're forecasting rain next week. It looks like we may get a good amount. Why?" Jim answered.

"We're thinking about heading home," explained BJ.

Talk between them continued, and Lizzy and BJ decided they would head home in two days' time.

So, the next day it was around to say goodbye to everyone. BJ packed up the ute and tied it all down securely. On the way out of town they called into The Flats to say a final goodbye to Beth and Bree and Cody, and of course, Beth and Bree had gifts for them.

"Now, BJ, here is some food for the road … Oh, I'm going to miss you so much. You look after yourself and Lizzy and the little one. I love you, son," Beth said.

Hugging Beth, BJ said, "Thanks, Mum. I hope you'll come up to the station in the cooler months."

"I'd like that very much," Beth answered, her eyes full of tears.

Instead of making it a four-day trip, they decided to crack on and get home as soon as possible. On the third day they drove into Emu Station — they had been sharing the driving and had only stopped at a motel once. The sky was not the beautiful blue it would normally be, instead there were dark clouds and the air smelt like rain.

"Looks like we're arriving home at the right time," remarked BJ.

Jim jumped straight in and helped BJ to unload his ute, while Sue took Lizzy inside to the kitchen. While Sue busied herself making coffee she asked, "Lizzy, do you remember the talk we had about protection? I'm wondering if you had done anything about it?"

"Mum, everything happened so quickly between me and BJ that contraception was forgotten about. What was happening was so electric, and the feelings … oh, protection wasn't even thought of, if you know what I mean." Lizzy hugged her mum and added, "Even though Peanut was unplanned, he or she is very much wanted. We've spoken about it since though, and after I have Peanut I will be going on the pill," Lizzy said.

Sue smiled and replied, "I understand what you mean about the intensity of your feelings for one another, but now I have to help you to get a nursery together. Oh, and where are you planning on having Peanut? We'll have to contact the Flying Doctor to check on your progress in the meantime. You do realise that there's *no* horse riding, and *no* mustering for a year now."

"Mum, I realise that, and it is going to be hard for me to give those things up, but it will be worth it in the long run," Lizzy said while gently rubbing her belly.

After days of rain, Jim and BJ checked the creek. "Holy hell, look at that!" Jim remarked, shocked.

"We just got back home in time … we were so lucky. The river level is way up, there's no going out now," BJ said, looking at the fast-flowing dirty water of the Cooee River.

"Sue, are you on air? Over," Jim spoke into the radio. "Yes, Jim, I'm here … what's up?" Sue asked.

"We're flooded in, the river is almost up to eight metres on the post, and it's flowing fast. Over and out," Jim advised.

Suddenly, Jim's neighbour—who was upstream on the river—called him on the radio. "Jim, you there? It's Collins Station here."

"Col, how are you? How much rain you had over there?" Jim asked.

"We're all fine. We got a downpour yesterday morning. It filled the rain gauge in about two hours, so we're flooded in as well. The weather report is saying we're in for more heavy rain. You look after yourself down there," Col said, and they finished the conversation.

"Welcome to the north in the wet, BJ," Jim said, smiling. "We better check on things around the property to make sure everything is okay. We'll definitely have to move the trucks up to the shed near the main house. Looks like Old Jimmie was right about the rain." Jim called up two of the workers who had already returned to Emu Station to go and move all the trucks up to the main house.

That night at dinner Jim mentioned to Sue that they should look for another worker as Lizzy would not be working next year. This brought a few sharp words from Lizzy, "I'm not dead, Dad, I can still do plenty of jobs. I am the vet, remember."

"Girly, you are not riding any horse or going on a muster. If someone is with you then you can check the horses. This is not open for debate," Jim's voice was firm but caring. "What do you say, BJ?"

"Jim, I've already spoken with Lizzy about no riding, and no mustering from now on. But you know your daughter. Me, I would prefer Lizzy to help Sue. Anyway, in the next few months she is going to be … hmm … bigger. You know what I mean, Peanut is growing fast." BJ answered while gently rubbing Lizzy's belly.

"I love you, girly, but after the bull incident, I worry about you and I don't want you hurt again." The love and concern in Jim's voice was obvious, "So, you help Mum around the house, but if I need you to look at something, you know vet-wise, then that would be okay. Your life will change when Peanut arrives."

Sue and Lizzy got to work fixing up the nursery, and because they were flooded in they shopped online for what was needed. They had contacted the Flying Doctor about Lizzy's pregnancy and the doctor had already flown in to do a pre-natal checkup. The doctor gave them a list of items needed so Lizzy could give birth on the station instead of going to hospital.

One day Sue was looking online at car seats for Peanut. "Lizzy, just wondering … are you keeping your car or are you planning on getting another one?"

"We're keeping my car and at the moment BJ is keeping his ute. We were going to get a new ute for BJ, but we decided saving money to spend on Peanut is more important. Besides, my Landcruiser Sahara is nearly brand new and it hasn't done that many miles," Lizzy said, and then she started to laugh, "BJ has never actually seen my car. I can't wait to see his face when he sees it for the first time."

Sue enquired, "Have you thought about a date for the wedding, love?"

"Well, at first we thought we'd get married this year, but now that there's a baby on the way, we're going to leave it until next year, when I can actually fit into a wedding dress," Lizzy explained and they both laughed at that.

The rain fell for days and days, and the river broke its banks in many places. Jim and BJ checked the river every few days, and Jim remarked that he had not seen the river this high for years.

By early February the river level had fallen and roads were open again, so the workers started to return to the station. Cookie had hitched a flight in with a neighbour who was flying back to his station, so he was already getting the cookhouse organised. One morning Jim turned up at the cookhouse.

"Well, welcome back everyone, hope you all had a good Christmas," Jim began. "As you know, this year we had rain, but the river broke its banks which means riding and checking things before the first muster. Also, we have a few changes this year. We have a new bloke starting next week. He comes off a station near Bandicoot River, and he has a lot of experience with mustering."

The door of the cookhouse opened and BJ and Lizzy walked in. Everyone said hi to them and then fell silent with their mouths open. Jim, BJ, and Lizzy laughed at the blokes' reaction.

"You can now see why the young bloke has been

employed. Yes, BJ and Lizzy are expecting. When is the big day, BJ?" Jim asked.

"Lizzy is due around the 17th of August," he answered.

"So, Lizzy is out for the year, and both BJ and I won't be on a muster around that time either, so Harry will be in charge then," Jim explained.

The months went by quickly, and work on the station continued. BJ was present every time the Flying Doctor did a pre-natal check on Lizzy.

"BJ, can you help me please?" Lizzy asked one day.

"What can I do for you?" questioned BJ.

"I can't bend down to pick up anything. Can you help me with this box please? Just put it on the bench there." Lizzy was frustrated that she couldn't do certain things because Peanut had grown so big. Jim even joked about how she walked now… in a loving way, of course.

It was now the 16th of August, and the weather had been odd all day. The morning started off humid and hot, the sky was its usual bright blue, but by lunch time the clouds started to roll in.

"Mum have you seen the clouds? I don't like the look of them," Lizzy said pointing at them.

"Hmm … I think we're in for a big storm," Sue said with a worried look on her face. Lizzy asked why.

"We had a storm the night before both you and Peter were born. My grandmother always said that a storm will bring on a baby if it is due. Have you had any back pain at all, or felt unusually uncomfortable?" Sue asked her.

"Funny you should say that. I woke up this morning and my back was aching but I put it down to the fact that I must have slept in an unusual position. And lately I can't seem to settle, all I want to do is walk," Lizzy admitted.

Sue had a surprised and worried look on her face. She knew what was happening. She radioed the Flying Doctor for advice and she radioed for Jim and BJ to come to the main house. It was time. They made it back to the main house just before the storm hit.

The storm crashed into Emu Station, bringing with it booming thunder, bolts of lightning and driving rain. Sue was in contact with the Flying Doctor by radio all night and early the next morning, after the storm had passed, the plane arrived at the station.

The Flying Doctor Service flew in just before 6 am, and the doctor and nurse attended to Lizzy, with BJ by her side. Jim kept walking up and down the hallway and out along the verandah. A nervous granddad, while Sue kept herself busy by cooking.

At 7 am on the 17th of August—Lizzy's due date— Peanut made his entrance into the world at Emu Station. Lizzy and BJ had decided not to find out the sex of the baby, they had wanted to be surprised.

Shortly after the baby's arrival an excited BJ entered the kitchen. "We have a boy!" he announced. Pats on the back from a smiling Jim and a hug from Sue who had happy tears in her eyes. Both proud grandparents. They followed BJ down the hallway to see a glowing Lizzy sitting up in bed, holding a small bundle.

"Mum and Dad, we would like you to meet your grandson." Lizzy said looking at the perfect baby in her arms.

"Have you decided on a name for him yet?" asked Jim, in between his tears.

"Yes, we have. We're not calling him Peanut anymore, this is Paul James Benjamin O'Brien," Lizzy said, beaming.

About the Author

BIANCA TODD

Bianca Todd writes from the heart and draws on her own experience of living and working on the land to create rich and full-bodied stories. Her first book, *Love After Dutchman's Road*, took the reader on a romantic adventure set against the spectacular backdrop of rural Australia.

In her second book, *Love In The Outback*, Bianca again explores themes from her own life experience and weaves them into a steamy and authentic Australian romantic story.

These days Bianca lives a quiet life in Queensland, Australia, where she writes to continue her own healing journey, and to inspire others to live their best life.

Acknowledgements

To Deborah Fay at Disruptive Publishing, thank you again for all your help, advice, and wisdom in getting my second romance novel published. Thank you for believing in me; I would not dream of engaging any other publishing consultant.

Words cannot adequately express my gratitude, my admiration, and my thanks to Jo Scott for her patience, advice, and assistance in editing my manuscript. The guidance, the feedback sessions, and all the moral support she has given me throughout editing my two books has been invaluable.

Jo's expertise has made my life so much easier as an author, and she has taught me so much through the process. Again thank you for working your magic. I would highly recommend Jo to any author.

To Casey Bahara for the beautiful cover image. The image depicts exactly what the story is about. Thank you so much.

www.ingramcontent.com/pod-product-compliance
Lightning Source LLC
Chambersburg PA
CBHW070314190726
48291CB00013B/1292